Bijoya Sawian is a translator and writer who lives in Shillong and Dehradun. She studied at Seng Khasi High School and Loreto Convent in Shillong, and did her Masters in English at Miranda House, Delhi, after graduating in English Literature from Lady Shri Ram College.

Her works essentially deal with the life and culture of the Khasi community of Northeast India. *The Teachings of Elders, Khasi Myths, Legends and Folktales* and *About One God* are three of several books that she has translated from Khasi into English. Several institutes of repute, including the Sahitya Akademi and the Institute of Folklore Studies, Bhopal, have published her short stories and critical essays.

Her original works in English include *A Family Secret and Other Stories.*

ALSO BY BIJOYA SAWIAN

A Family Secret and Other Stories (2014)
The Main Ceremonies of the Khasis (pub. Vivekananda Institute of Culture, Guwahati, 2012, 2018)

PRAISE FOR *SHADOW MEN*

'From its opening lines, the angst and anger, sadness and bitternesses, suspicion and fear of a time when hope and tragedy walked hand in hand on the streets of Shillong seep through the pages of *Shadow Men*. Through simple strokes, Bijoya Sawian, who grew up in the city, grips the attention of readers with her detailed stories of those who lived, died and loved in a beautiful land hollowed by anxieties, violence and cautionary tales.'

—Sanjoy Hazarika, author of *Strangers in the Mist: Tales of War*, and *Strangers No More: New Narratives*

'Bijoya Sawian knows her Shillong well and it is evident in her debut novel. The author aptly captures the mood, the weather and the people of the place in her prose...Being a Shillongite, I could almost put real-life faces to the characters of the novel.'

—Soumyadip in Network18

'In crisp, everyday conversations, the festering wounds of a splintered hill state are laid bare—the downside of the matrilineal system, the disconnect with mainstream India, crippling unemployment, drug and alcohol addiction, corrupt politicians—you get it all.'

—*Assam Tribune*

SHADOW MEN

A NOVEL AND TWO STORIES

Bijoya Sawian

SPEAKING
TIGER

SPEAKING TIGER BOOKS LLP
125 A Shahpur Jat, Near Asiad Village
New Delhi 110049

This edition published in paperback by Speaking Tiger Books 2019

ISBN: 978-93-89692-11-2
eISBN: 978-93-89692-12-9

10 9 8 7 6 5 4 3 2 1

Typeset in Adobe Garamond Pro by SÜRYA, New Delhi
Printed at ...

For Mother Nives and Aneeta Dey

CONTENTS

SHADOW MEN

Prologue

They say that when you are alive you are actually dreaming and when you die, you awaken. That summer was like a dream with the wakefulness of life, that summer in the faraway hill town where I grew up long ago, so long ago it seems a past life almost. There amidst the vicissitudes of Nature I found myself dreaming a dream so frightening it woke me up forever.

1

Ghostlike, the mist floated up from the gorge below, encircling the gardener's cottage and the trees, seeping languidly through the flowering shrubs. It climbed up the hedge of azaleas and gently made its way past the tall monsoon grass. It parted slightly and I noticed three figures climbing up the west-facing slope. Something about the way they moved caught my eye for it wasn't the easy, after-work saunter of household staff. They were quick and furtive yet clumsy, clearly unfamiliar with the terrain and the path that zigzagged through the plum and pear orchard.

The mist thickened, now rising quickly to form an impenetrable curtain And then suddenly it broke to expose three young men in the dimly-lit verandah of the gardener's cottage below. One of them had a gun. Rooted to the ground and cold with fright I watched his sinister silhouette.

While the other two were leaning against the wooden posts that shouldered the leaky tin roof of the verandah, the man with the gun entered the cottage. The two looked around with an air of seeming nonchalance. I thought that one of them had a face blotchy with white leucoderma patches but I couldn't be sure. Just at that moment the phone rang.

2

'Hello.'

'Hi! Is that you, Raseel?'

'Yes…'

'Hi! Why, why are you sounding so distant? Can't recognize my voice or what?'

'Of course, Vinny, it's the line and the distance, sorry!'

'Oh, okay! Listen, I would like two more of these cane sets from Nagaland. One for Chandigarh and the other I will sell at double the price, good idea don't you think? It'll pay for my transport unless Gurbir Chacha does the needful through the army. This set I bought last time is looking so good. Hello Ras, Hello! Hello!'

The mist swirled into the hall along with a gust of wind, dislodging a golf cap from the wooden hat stand. I shifted on my feet uncomfortably, not knowing how to respond to Vinny's chatter about the cane sets from Nagaland. It was then that I heard a shot followed by several cracker-like bursts.

'Vinny, I'll call you back in the evening—bye—yes, yes, don't worry.'

In a flash I was back at the window. Three figures were tumbling down the slope through the mist, carrying what seemed, from where I stood, like a long duffle bag. Out of the cottage a fourth figure emerged, walking quickly through the mist down to the stream at the foot of the hillock. Just before he disappeared from sight, the slim, medium-built figure in a maroon shirt looked back at the cottage once. The mist was thickening and I thought I saw another figure emerging from the cottage when the phone rang again.

I ran back. By the time I reached it was dead.

3

On the hill opposite, a tall white house with windows like tired, hollow eyes rose above a cluster of small hill cottages, red-roofed, innocent. Inside, the man moved away from a window. He put down his binoculars and lit a cigarette and offered one to his companion.

'There was a woman at the window. I don't know how long she had been there though.'

'What? We've had it! I thought everyone was out of town. How could this happen? Wasn't it quite certain that nobody would be there? How is this possible?'

'Stop panicking, Ksan. Never panic. There's no problem that cannot be solved. I've got the phone cut. The rest we will see.'

Then he dialled a number.

4

I rushed to the kitchen. It was quiet, at peace, a picture of perfect domestic bliss. It was bathed in soft golden light…the remains of the day were glowing and lace curtains were billowing in the wind.

Kmie U Flin had prepared tea for me. It was five o'clock and Shillong teatime. On the pale blue tray cloth with a sprinkling of pink and lilac flowers on four sides, were two cups, a matching milk jug, sugar bowl and a teapot all in pale pink.

I stared at Kmie U Flin to see if there was any trace of panic or worry but there was none. Very quietly, as she always did, she said, 'Pour yourself a cup of tea before it gets cold. Come, Kong Raseel, enjoy your tea.'

I continued to look at her, confused and wondering if the events of the past few minutes were but a figment of my imagination. There was Kmie U Flin shuffling around as she always did. She had been brought many years ago as a live-in domestic help as was normally done in all aristocratic families. She had four, no…three children all named with great élan after Hollywood stars by her husband, the late Kwinton Lyngdoh. So there was Errol Flynn Marbaniang, James Dean Marbaniang, and the youngest, Sophia Lamon Marbaniang. The Khasi touch for Sophia was probably because she was a girl and a 'khatduh'. Tragedy struck, however, and Sophia died of dysentery as a child and all Plisina Marbaniang wanted to do was leave her village of Mawsynram forever. Marbaniang is one of the noble clans of the West Khasi Hills, this was also taken into account when she moved in.

'What are you staring at, Kong Raseel? Is the tray cloth stained?' Kmie U Flin stood in front of me with worry in her eyes, a plate of cucumber sandwiches in one hand and Mahari cookies in the other, fifteen rupees a pound when I was in school long ago.

'No, the tray cloth is not stained, Kmie U Flin.' I started laughing. Obsession with cleanliness is an endearing Khasi trait.

'Come, let's have tea, Kmie U Flin, here have this jam tart—yum!' I said, trying desperately to cling to normalcy.

Kmie U Flin had always been treated with respect because of her age and background. There was always a guarded pretence of equality with her by everyone in the family. No one disturbed the magnanimity and genuine affection, which the loyal domestic never abused. On her part she never forgot her place in one of the wealthiest families of these hills, belonging to a clan that once ruled the hima of Mawsynram, the place which not so long ago had recorded rainfall even higher than nearby Cherrapunjee.

'Kmie U Flin,' I said as she settled down on a mula near me with her mug of tea, 'do people around here carry guns?'

'Guns? Yes, yes the police and those CRP men… wherever they are patrolling,' she replied, biting into the jam tart, then she added, 'Militants too and naughty boys but not openly, of course. That's what Robart tells me. I am so happy the tray cloth is not stained. Is the tea all right?'

Kmie U Flin wasn't pretending; all she was worried about at that point in time was something going wrong with her perfectly laid-out tea. Obviously Aunty Rosamon had schooled her well: tea should be consumed serenely, in the right place with the right conversation and the appropriate china cups and other accessories. Why should I spoil it all with my own neurosis, spoil this idyll, I ruminated, as Kmie U Flin brought out a plain cake from the oven, freshly baked.

Such an immense relief to be away from Delhi where a glassy stare would have rushed Renu Masi and Cousin Sonia to the phone to talk in hushed tones to my psychiatrist, Minna Jaiswal, about what they would have termed the 'latest development'. Minna Jaiswal came into my life three years ago and weaned me away from dismal depression after the murder of my parents in Delhi by their domestic help. Now it was so refreshing to be somewhere else where a blank look was simply associated with a stain on a tray cloth.

I shivered as the mist swirled in through an open window and the lace curtains fluttered like battered butterflies. How I wished my old school friend, Aila, and her husband Aibor, were here with me! Aila and Aibor were my hosts—it was their house I was staying at. But they were away on a cruise, and there was a whole week ahead, maybe more, for their return. I wrapped my shawl tightly around me.

'Kmie U Flin, please close the window,' I shivered.

'Yes, yes, mosquitoes will get in, that's the problem with the summer.'

'Kmie U Flin, where is the PCO?'

'The what, Kong Raseel?'

'The telephone booth...'

'Phone...? It's in the hall. There's an extension here too.'

'The phone is dead.'

'Oh! That happens once in a while. It'll get it fixed once Robart comes. He has a mobile. He'll call.'

'Where's Robert?'

Robert Nongrum was Aibor's cousin. He also worked for the family and Kmie U Flin looked upon him as a son.

'He has gone to buy some fruits, pineapples are excellent in this season and he's bringing some pork too. I will make doh iong for you. I know you like it, or would you prefer chicken, there's some in the fridge...'

'Kmie U Flin, tell me who lives in the cottage in the orchard?'

'Sures and Rabi. I hope Robart doesn't forget my kwai and tympew.'

Sures and Rabi. I froze. The names clearly suggested that they were 'dkhars', plainsmen but I still persisted, hoping against hope.

'Yes,' Kmie U Flin replied cheerily, 'Wonderful boys from Bihar. Our boys don't work half as hard as them. Always taking leave and in a day they take four, five breaks, smoking their pipes or lying on their backs staring at the sky as if...'

So Suresh and Ravi were dkhars, Biharis. 'Kmie U Flin, please could you call Suresh and Ravi. I want to talk to them. And there's nothing wrong with staring at the sky, it's the most divine experience...but please, go and call Suresh and Ravi first.' I could hear the panic in my words and feel the beginnings of that familiar throbbing in my head. I rushed to a window and took three deep, long breaths. I learnt that at a yoga center in Rishikesh.

'Kong Raseel, what is it that you would like to know? They are gardeners, they have nothing to do with the house. Robart will come soon and do something about the phone. Have your tea, another cup. You should always sip it calmly, only then will it be of any benefit. Nowadays...'

'Yes, yes, Kmie U Flin, nobody realizes all this nowadays, the right thoughts, the right conversation, the right surroundings, even the right colour clothes during teatime. Come, come, let us go down to the gardener's cottage. I feel I need a short walk. I'll have more tea with everything absolutely perfect and the way Aunty Rosamon would have liked but that comes later. Come.'

There must have been a certain firmness in my voice and resolve in the way I stood up because she stopped, paused, did a turnabout and walked out into the mist without saying a word. I followed her rather guiltily. I had never been so curt to her ever before. I was relieved when I heard her starting to hum softly, an easy familiar tune that floated through the air like a wandering cloud.

I watched her digging her hand into the ubiquitous cloth bag that hung on her right shoulder across her bosom down to her left hip, for some kwai. My throat knotted and my eyes smarted. It took me back thirty years—Mom, Dad, lambent sunshine and laughing Khasi maids, Jenny, Christina and little Annie, Jenny's daughter.

5

'Why didn't you tell us that there was a house guest?' the man slurred.

'She wasn't expected so soon. Apparently, Kong Aila was not sure she… ' the man replied and was cut short.

'How close is she to the family?'

'Very close, Strong, very close.'

'Shit! Let us clear our heads before we tell the Boss. I have to work it out anyway.'

Then both of them sank into the sofas and grabbed some much-needed sleep.

6

Kmie U Flin stood on her toes, tall enough for her voice to travel over the hedge of azaleas that stretched along the road above the orchard.

'Sures ko Sures, Rabi ko rabi,' she called out through the falling light and receding day, as a light drizzle suddenly showered from the sky. I was shaking and my teeth chattered. I took deep breaths as I herded all the negative feelings into a distant corner of my mind. I echoed Kmie U Flin,'Suresh ko Suresh, Ravi ko Ravi.'

We were greeted by a deep silence. It was so quiet, as quiet as the beginning of Time. I wrapped my arms around myself, trying to control my heart which was beating fast like a bird in panic. I could feel fear creeping in.

'Where are these boys? They don't normally go out on weekdays. Even on Sundays they go out only during the day. I will tell Robart to give them a good lecture. This is no way to behave. Anyway, there's nothing to worry about.'

Even as she said it, I knew Kmie U Flin, sensing my fear, was trying to reassure me.

'Should I...?' but before I could articulate what I wanted to desperately, the lights went off.

'Come, Kong Raseel, we will go and have some tea.' She spoke loudly as if darkness made men deaf but more to convince herself that all was well.

As we trudged back my head sat like an enormous

boulder on my shoulders, silent, unmoving. Is this all a dream? Maybe Minna Jaiswal was right. I exaggerated events just to reassure myself that worse things could happen than your parents being murdered, butchered by a man they trusted. At a placid lunch at the Delhi Gym when Minna and cousin Vinny and I suddenly erupted into a heated discussion on trust, I remembered commenting that trusting was a criminal act because of the gigantic responsibility with which it burdened the object of trust. Anything that weighed down a human being was a crime worse than all the crimes ever enumerated. That evening I was prescribed a new strip of medicines.

'Come, Kong Raseel,' Kmie U Flin was saying. 'I will make some pure, light Darjeeling with lemon. It's very refreshing. Oh! See Robart has come…'

The headlights of a car pierced through the darkness that was slowly filtering in. The car purred to a halt at the porch and Robert tumbled out carrying two loaded bags of shopping.

'Robart, the lights have gone off, the phone is dead and Sures and Rabi are not in their rooms,' Kmie U Flin rattled off the complaints while offering to help with the bags.

I thought I sensed a tense anger in Robert but I wasn't sure for his reply was casual and carefree.

'Oh, don't worry. They must be watching a film on TV. They are young boys; they may have gone out to visit their cousins who are working not far from here.'

'Where? I've never heard of these cousins,' Kmie U Flin interjected, sounding a little piqued.

'You have never heard of so many things, Meisan—come, let us go in. This drizzle is treacherous. You have not experienced it yet, Kong, but you will. We'll get wet and yet not feel cold and tomorrow we'll be in bed with fever,' said Robert, calm and collected, holding Kmie U Flin by her shoulders.

'Robert, have you had tea?' I asked

'Yes, Kong Raseel. At Bah Ellis.'

'He means Kong Pat's, this rogue,' said Kmie U Flin, smiling, snuggling up to Robert like a fond parent. 'There is no harm in admiring beauty but remember she is married, Robart.'

'All right, all right, Meisan. Bah Ellis was still at work but the beautiful Kong Pat didn't serve me tea either, her mother did. On top of that she forgot to put sugar, she added too much milk and I could do nothing about it. But, yes, she served me crisp pyllon shroin and I have brought some for Kong Raseel to have with her morning tea.'

'Thank you so much, Robert.'

'Now we will all have…'

'No, Kmie U Flin, no more tea. We will all have wine. Ok, ok, folks I know it's not done normally, but I have come from faraway after a long time so let's have a party! Aibor and Aila will understand. Don't worry. I will explain it to them. Promise! I really want to chat and relax.'

Robert picked up the local paper and started reading it. Kmie U Flin on the other hand pulled back her shoulders, put up her little nose and very proudly said to me, 'Kong Aila does give me brandy when it gets very cold, it really helps. Unfortunately, I now have this sugar disease so she stopped giving me except once in awhile. Robart, bring your glass and you can have it in your room. I will have it before going to bed, in my room.'

'No, no,' I interrupted, amused and yet horrified by her plan. 'We will not have wine separately. We will sit together wherever you all feel comfortable and enjoy it together. I want to chat, yes, I just want to chat.'

Two pairs of eyes stared back at me. One pair was filled with surprise and affection, the other with suspicion.

7

'The woman from Delhi, damn her, is already looking for them.'

'Shit!'

'I believe nobody in the house knew about this woman's arrival.'

'How can that be?'

'I believe she said she wanted to give Bah Aibor and Kong Aila a surprise when they return from their trip.'

'Hah! Surprise!'

'She's on some nostalgic trip. She grew up here, studied with Kong Aila. They are good friends.'

'Shut UP,' shouted Strong. 'Gossiping like a woman. Let's focus on the problem—let us presume that this woman saw everything.'

'I am as worried, Strong.'

'Nothing to worry as such. I have the remedy as always.'

'I don't like the look in your eyes, she could be some VIP's wife, daughter, sister and…'

'I am not thinking what you are thinking, dumbo,' Strong growled and bared his teeth in a sinister grin.

8

I knew I was doing everything wrong. Immediately after I heard the gunshot and realized that the phone was dead, I should have run up the hill, out of the gate, up the second slope and traversed the country lane to reach the market and the nearest PCO. I should have called the police, the other school friends in town, Aila's father and brothers. They could have contacted Aibor who was, along with Aila, sightseeing in China, viewing the only 'wonder of the world' that they hadn't seen, the Great Wall.

On that August evening, however, everything seemed to alternate between nightmare and dream and with those around me so calm, so casual and dismissive, my reaction seemed totally out of proportion.

I went over the scene again and again, the attire of the men, their build and features, their body language. I did the same with the lone boy who fled from the scene, after what I thought were gunshots. The way he walked away almost in slow motion.

I guess I felt foolish talking about all this because I simply wasn't sure. For quite a while after my parents' murder I was prone to hallucinations. Minna confirmed it. It was the scariest period of my life. I certainly didn't want a relapse. If I didn't speak about something I could sit on it but giving words to a thought somehow gave it flesh and blood. Besides, there didn't seem to be a crisis here at all.

Honestly that was what I decided as I sat in that green, tin-roofed hill bungalow, mist all around, lace curtains billowing in the breeze, quiet everywhere.

9

In a hotel room in an upmarket locality the men sat sipping Peter Scot. There was a third person dressed in corduroy trousers and a tweed coat and three boys in jeans and jackets.

'Anyway,' the man said, adjusting his elegant tie around his slim neck that held a refined face with Mongolian features. 'What did the woman see? Three men carrying a bag and another one leaving with a suitcase. That's all. What's so abnormal? They have all disappeared after the robbery. That's all. There are bloodstains in the room… the incident will be in the news for days. That was what we wanted. As for the gun shots, that Marwari family was bursting crackers all day. That one shot couldn't have been that loud, what did you use?' he addressed a young leather-jacketed man, who was puffing imperiously on an India King.

The boy shuffled uncomfortably and answered, 'An AK-47.'

'Hmm…anyway, as Bah Strong said we should not panic. All that is expected of you all is absolute loyalty. We think, we plan, we tell you what to do. Ksan, did you find out more details about this woman?'

'No. She seems harmless enough, innocent, but snoopy, also strange. She hasn't alerted anyone. She has only told those two at home.'

'Who's the cop who is investigating?'

'We don't know yet…'

'You don't know yet? It's almost five hours now and you don't know yet? Where's my mobile? You young ones may leave now. See that tonight's plan doesn't turn out to be another free movie show.'

Taking a huge gulp from his glass he punched furiously on the numbers of his mobile.

The three boys walked out of the room to rejoin their companions in the waiting car outside, a common and innocent-looking old, green Gypsy.

10

By the time Robert came up from his suite, positioned at one end of the main staff quarters, I was ready with the wine and banana chips brought from a corner shop in Delhi.

Robert had spruced up and looked good. I had always found him handsome. He was after all, not only Aibor's second or third cousin but also of mixed parentage. His father was a Sindhi businessman, whose Sindhi wife wisely overlooked her husband's local liaison, for the gains in this alien territory were many and lucrative. He moved on from his Khasi wife as soon as he was established. He provided for her well and bought her a three-bedroom house in Malki and a small shop below in the little marketplace. Primrose Nongrum was not happy for she had begun to get used to her husband, to love him, in fact, but she was far too proud to ask him to stay. She had too much self-respect to confront him about his betrayal. He hadn't even told her he was married. She didn't know he had a wife tucked away in Bombay. She brought up her son with dignity and pushed Sunil Sindhwani out of her life forever. Later, she remarried and had two more children, a son and a daughter, but the marriage did not last long.

Robert sat on the mula a little away from the fire. 'It's warm,' he remarked, and it was but Kmie U Flin had lit it just for my sake. She remembered that I enjoyed sitting near the fire and it always made me feel wonderful. She had kept a chair for me, a perfectly crafted cane chair with a soft cushion with a satin cover. I pushed it gently away. 'Please, Kmie U Flin, just this once,' I said, and dragged a mula right next to them before anyone could protest. Then I turned to Robert.

'Robert, now tell me what all has been happening with you, we have thirty years to catch up on…Oh, well…maybe let's just hear some stories, stories you tell your children like the ones we used to hear as kids, folk tales. Remember that heart-wrenching tale, Sier Lapalang? Lord Mountbatten wanted the folk song to be sung at his funeral. Kmie U Flin was so good with all that but she's busy. Let's just talk, anything you feel like.'

Kmie U Flin, who had taken her glass to the kitchen, peeped in and acknowledged my remembering with the sweetest of smiles. The gesture put me at ease. I wanted so much to be reassured.

'Stories?' Robert laughed. 'Firstly my children all live with their mother. She left me and remarried some years ago. Even when we were all together, where was the time for stories? It was TV and more TV, once their homework and household chores were done.'

'What do they watch, Robert?'

'Sports, cartoons but most of all Hindi serials and films.'

'Hindi films?'

'Yes, my kids didn't go to an English-medium school so it's not English films, AXN, Star World, V Channel and all that. It's Hindi films and songs.'

'Strange, isn't it, Robert, that there's all this hype

about outsiders, plainsmen. I would imagine that people here would not accept anything from the mainland, 'India' as they call it.'

'Kong Raseel, nobody considers Amitabh Bachchan, Aamir Khan, Madhuri Dixit and Preity Zinta dkhars. They are from the skies, the stars.'

'How about asking them to come here and talk about, say—national unity and all that, about the true feelings of the mainlanders about how we are one people, one country...'

"The true feelings, Kong? We all know what the true feelings are. Let's face it: the dkhars will always look down on us tribals.'

'Robert, in India everyone looks down on everyone, the Brahmins turn up their noses at the Kshatriyas, the Kshatriyas look down on the Kayasths, the Kayasths on the Vaishyas and it just goes on. My parents were both Sikhs but my mother had to rebel when she married my father because he wasn't a Jat Sikh. One has to be confident of one's worth as a human being and just believe, believe in a world where the mind is without fear and the head is held high—remember Tagore?'

Robert looked down at his toes. My eyes wandered away to the window. On the opposite hill something was burning, the flames leaping up almost playfully as if it was a game. But I knew it wasn't.

11

The woman watched the fire slowly minimizing into grey dust and a monsoon wind sweeping it all away. She chewed her kwai noisily, as she lay sprawled across a coarsely carved divan in her large drawing room littered with kitschy vases and collectibles. So typical.

The phone rang. She picked it up.

'Is it over?' the man on the other end asked.

'Yes, you can come back whenever you wish.'

'Did you inform the police, the rangbah shnong, the press and the neighbours?'

'Yes, yes, they were all here. Bah Heh is handling them like a good son. My absence is overlooked because of my blood pressure and gout.'

'Ok. What's for dinner?'

'Pork in boiled cabbage, Tungtap chutney…'

'Good, I'll start off after an hour or so. If anyone else rings up to inquire, please sound suitably agitated. Remember I am in Ron's farm out of reach by telephone and I left my mobile behind.'

'I know, I know. When do we get a new car?'

But the man had hung up.

12

Kmie U Flin stood rooted by the window, speechless. Robert kept sipping his wine calmly as if nothing was happening. When I could bear it no longer I asked.

'What's happening? What are they burning?'

'A minister's car.'

'Why?'

'There's an agitation against the government about seats for studies and jobs. The Garos don't deserve that many seats, the vacancies are never filled, they go waste, we deserve more.'

'More?'

'Yes, Khasis and Jaintias 60 percent and Garos 30 percent, and the rest 10 percent.'

'Oh?'

'Kong, please relax. It's all very complicated so don't try to understand.'

'Don't listen to him. Robart, please stop it. It must be an accident. Why should they burn Bah Jus' car? He's a good man, a good MLA. He's not the chief minister.'

'He's part of the cesspool…and by the way, Meisan, he's apparently trying very hard to become the chief minister. How would you know? For forty-odd years you have been closeted here in the lap of luxury. How would you know what is happening beyond these four walls?' Robert shouted.

Kmie U Flin gasped, her hands flew to her mouth and her frail body sank into my chair and she began to sob. I held her close, as my eyes captured the sight of smoke billowing across the hillside and my ears caught the sound of water being sprayed, like waves on a moonlit shore.

Against it all was silhouetted the chiselled face of Robert Nongrum, head held high, mouth calm, eyes resolute.

'Let's have dinner, Kmie U Flin. Yes, you go and heat it, thank you.'

When she had disappeared into the kitchen, I went and sat next to Robert.

'Robert, I know saying "why don't people just talk things out" is easy but still there must be some solution.'

'How can there be a solution when nobody is articulating the problem? Some don't even know it.'

'But you said it's about seats and jobs.'

'That's what's floating on top. The dkhars are usurping our jobs, they are stealing our women—get them out, kill them—the Garos are letting the seats go waste, they could never fill them—protest.'

'So that's it?'

'No. That is not it. Over the years all that has increased and multiplied is the number of protestors! That is the only progress made. They come from the villages where there is no development, because the MLA couldn't care less. They come here and realize that it isn't all that easy, well, at least for most of them so they turn to all sorts of crimes or they simply drink, drug and sell themselves…in different ways. Now, of course, there's a new Employment Exchange.'

'Oh, really?'

'Yes, don't you know? The work is very easy, the pay excellent. Extort, burn, kill, ask no questions. "If you've got guts, here's the gun, follow our orders and collect your paycheck." That's it, Kong Raseel.'

'Robert, for God's sake, what are you saying?'

'I am saying what the truth is as one sees it. Go a little deeper and then one gets to know the larger picture, the deeper truth, and the reality. That is when one faces the only truth. Deep down there it stares you in the face like a demon, unmoving.'

'What is the demon saying, Robert? Does it have a voice?'

'Sure it does. It speaks through the horrors that erupt all the time. Everyone hears but no one listens. Look, Kong Raseel, let me not beat around the bush. The men here are in a terrible state. We are sad, we are desperate and all these terrible emotions stem from that. We own nothing, not a patch of land is given by the family, not a pie. Even our children belong to their mother. Unless one gets a government job what does one do? Nothing! We are fighting for equal distribution of wealth but till that comes through most of us just float around like scum in a stagnant well. No money, no sense of self-worth, no nothing. Nothing! Yeah—that's it. That's the truth that no one understands.'

Tears welled up in his eyes, red as live coals. He squeezed the wine glass. It broke and the blood stained the glass red and his shirt, trousers, socks and the Tibetan rug on the floor.

I understood. I knew that the Khasis, Jaintias and Garos belong to a matrilineal society. The lineage is taken from the mother. The daughters inherit, with the youngest as the custodian of the major share of the property. Her parents live with her and so do any unmarried members of the family. The sons do not inherit but are supported by the family until they get jobs or get married and move out to their wives' homes. The maternal uncles were once much revered and they had the last word in all important decisions. In a world where money and status have replaced all values, this system, obviously, no longer worked.

I touched Robert's shoulder. Framed against the door opposite was Kmie U Flin.

'What is he doing? What is he talking about? He has never talked like this before. Robart, what has happened, son?'

'No, he couldn't have because he said no one listens. Oh! Kmie U Flin, don't look so sad.'

I started to cry. The tears flowed like the bursting of a dam. And I let them. It was exactly what I needed.

I had never felt so scared.

13

'Bah Jus' wife apparently didn't show enough fear…or panic.'

'What do you expect of her! She is a fool. Anyway no one suspected. There was plenty of commotion.'

'Yeah! As long as this CM goes and Bah Jus comes in he may be able to do something about the quotas…'

'Yeah…but let's not fool ourselves, Ksan. Who cares about all that as long as we get our way.'

'Don't be so angry, Strong. What way, anyway?'

'Actually, I don't know, Ksan.'

14

'Kmie U Flin, what about Suresh and Ravi?'

'Robart…?'

'Their lights are off. They must be asleep. Kong Raseel, Meisan was telling you about her cousin, Bah Hekstar. Yes, he did marry the youngest daughter of the family. Yes, he is highly respected, yes, he is loved, yes, he's happy. You know why? Because he moved in as a rich man. A successful smuggler as a young man, he turned to trade and became respectable and now his children are all professionals. It all comes down to economics. He is a much-respected mama in his sister's home and a revered father in his wife's. But how many people can be successful smugglers and bootleggers? It's as difficult as getting a government job! You want to start something on your own, where's the money? We can't even approach the bank because there's no guarantee. You tell your sisters and they pretend ignorance, some offer their sympathies. You turn to your parents and they give you a lecture on customs and the laws of inheritance. So one goes to one's room and drinks oneself to sleep, if one is married one goes to a bed, to a woman who really doesn't need you after a while.'

'Robart…'

'The men here are…well, see, first they were bewildered—like "what's happening?" so they pinpointed the problem, worked out this great big solution and we got a state of our own. We tried our best to make the government do something about it—but who listens once they are enthroned, huh? Still things were going wrong so they zeroed in on all the outsiders "because they are stealing our jobs, our women, our land." Except for those who had the money to pay, the rest had their houses burnt, their bodies battered. Many fled, some clung on, the Bengalis, Nepalis, Biharis and, of course, wealthy Marwaris, Sindhis, Sikhs. They stayed but they lived according to the new rules. Everyone knows his place. Yet things were still the same. No jobs, no opportunities. You don't know what it's like to go home and not be able put food on the table. So now it's become the Garos. These are all punching bags. Out of sheer frustration we punch, we shoot, we kill. I feel so and I think I am right. Every Khasi man feels so faltu, so completely and utterly helpless.'

'Robart, maternal uncles and brothers are highly respected in every Khasi home.'

'That was long ago, Meisan, before the priests replaced them. Who asks a mama for permission and all that stuff nowadays, unless he is someone? They ask the priest. Especially in homes like yours, Meisan, Christian homes.'

Kmie U Flin stared at Robert, speechless, unbelieving. I gathered her in my arms and gently stroked her head till she calmed down and started to cry.

I could feel the shock and sadness which I shared with her on that warm August evening in a hill town faraway.

15

'How many?'

'Five government cars—two jeeps, three Ambassadors and a private car.'

'Why?'

'Bah Jus' car. Just to...you know! No one should guess. After all he is an MLA and a member of the party. Now he'll able to function freely and his ministers will do the rest.'

'His ministers?'

'Yes, he's bought two of them. They will do the needful. That is what the Boss said.'

'And?'

'And strict instructions have been issued that we must show that this agitation is not ethnic or communal, it is simply anti-government. Law and order situation in a mess, the outsiders are feeling insecure and they will agitate against the CM. That's very important. I don't have to elaborate.'

'I know, I know.'

16

By the time I woke up the sun was high and strong, slanting into my room through the east-facing window fronted by pots of geraniums. There were loud, desperate knocks on my door. As I opened it, Titi, the daily help, flew into my room, almost dropping the morning tea tray. She was shaking like a leaf.

'Kong, Kong, Sures and Rabi have disappeared!'

'Why didn't you wake me up earlier?'

'Bah Robart said you need rest. Oh, Kong, the police have come, and so many others.'

I rushed to the bathroom and hugged myself tight. The nightmare had begun to surface again. I, too, began to shake like a leaf. I swallowed a Valium and poured myself a cup of tea. Titi sat on the mat on the floor and started to cry. I paced the room, not knowing what to do next. There was no escaping the truth now. I watched the sunbeams dancing on my quilt and my mind went blank.

'There's blood on the walls…'

'Where?'

'In the gardener's cottage, Kong. What is happening? I am feeling so scared. Oh, Kong!' and suddenly, she rushed towards me and clung to my legs like a leech. I was as scared as Titi and unhinged by this uncharacteristic show of emotion, so unlike a Khasi. I put my hand on her head. I felt completely marooned in an island of deep sadness and guilt.

The cop was scribbling furiously in his notebook when I went down. A chair had been brought out for him. He sat in the morning sun in the overgrown lawn in his starched uniform and shoes that shone like a mirror. A little away, in a separate group distinctly different in every way, sat the rangbah shnong, the locality headman, and a few neighbours and well-wishers. Aibor's two brothers arrived in their shining Esteems and I sighed with immense relief when I saw Aila's father, Uncle Rangshan, arriving in his superbly preserved Ambassador. I ran into his arms and hugged him tight. He had come alone. When Aunty Rosamon died, he had remarried and moved to his second wife's house. Aunty Binola was a childless widow from a good family, much to everyone's relief because Uncle Rangshan was an extremely attractive man and had a legion of admirers, most of them not so suitable.

The cop was questioning Robert.

'Around 8 a.m., I came up to clean the cars. Suresh normally helps me with it.I was surprised when he was not here. So I called out to him and Ravi too. When nobody responded, I went down to the cottage.'

'Before that you had no inkling of their absence? You are all in the same compound, Robert.'

'No, no, I knew nothing till I went down to the cottage this morning and realized that the boys were missing. I saw Suresh's pants and shirts and his suitcase in the room,' Robert answered without a moment's hesitation.

My heart stopped as I studied my neglected toes with

chipped nail polish that peeked out of my Marie Claire sandals. Robert had lied. He had put me in a fix. What was I supposed to do? I would go completely mad if I had to bottle up yesterday's events.

'Well,' hummed the cop, 'it seems like a simple case of robbery. The victim, Suresh, was killed. His friend was spared for some reason and fled. But who committed the crime? Or was it Ravi? That we will find out by and by. Yes, so Robert you are saying that Suresh was not planning to go on leave so all the salary money must have been in the suitcase which is now missing. I fear a murder most foul. I will inspect the cottage now. Tch! Tch! The law and order situation in the state has really worsened. Don't you think?'

Kmie U Flin sidled up to me and squeezing my hand, whispered, 'Don't worry. I don't know why he said what he said but I am not letting anyone cast aspersions on Rabi and Sures just like that,' and tidying her hair and jainkyrshah, she walked towards the cop. Uncle Rangshan was desperately trying to contact Aibor through a friend's son who worked in a hotel in Shanghai.

'Look, Bah,' Kmie U Flin said, 'I am quite sure that Rabi didn't rob and kill Sures. They loved each other like brothers. They worked together, stayed together, ate, drank and laughed together. They are from the same village!'

'Look, Kong, crime is not as simple as all that. Money is always a huge temptation. I deal with all this every day. Understand? And so far we have not established any facts anyway.'

Kmie U Flin glared at him but was rendered speechless. She had not met a cop before, ever. I decided to step in. For some reason the cop looked up and rose to his full height of five feet four inches and gave a small, brisk bow.

'Yes, Ma'am. You are?'

'I am Raseel Babbar. I am a childhood friend of Aila's. We were here in Loreto Convent, in the same class. I came here a few days ago from Delhi.' I shook his hand. Nice handshake, neither too hard nor too spongy.

'I see, I see,' he said chirpily and continued to stand. 'How do you like the weather? Raining a lot, no? How long…'

'I am used to it.'

'Yes, yes. How long are you staying?'

I found his question not only rude but disturbing, more disturbing than rude, actually.

'Officer, Kmie U Flin is absolutely correct. I, too, do not think it's a simple case of robbery. I also think both the boys are innocent. The one who has disappeared is not the perpetrator.'

'The what?'

'The criminal.'

'Really?' his eyes narrowed and he looked at me deep and hard. 'You have been here only three days.'

'Five days.'

'Ok, how can you be so sure about all this?'

'Last evening, just before dusk I saw one of the boys leaving the cottage with his belongings, well, a bag…'

'He was running?'

'No, he was walking away with a suitcase in his hand and he looked back at the cottage once and then carried on down the slope. He was not running. He didn't seem like a man on the run.'

'I see, I see. How do you know that he was carrying his belongings?'

'Ok, I don't know what he was carrying. So I am as ignorant as you are.' I smiled at him and he too flashed back his small, almost womanly, pearly white teeth. I continued undeterred, 'Before that three men had come to the cottage. One of them was armed. He went inside and the other two hung around in the verandah. One of them had leucoderma.'

I was hoping that would have the effect of a Hiroshima bomb but I was wrong. He simply nodded and wrote it down in his notebook and thanked me as if all I had done was give him information on the latest weather condition…not even an earthquake.

I think I stared at him with my mouth open. Inside I was screaming, 'Are we here to investigate a crime or nail an innocent boy?'

We walked away, Uncle Rangshan and I, to the comforting shade of an old chestnut tree. I took three deep breaths, chanting, 'Shanti, shanti, shanti.'

Uncle Rangshan put his hand gently on my shoulder and said, 'Yes, say your prayers.'

'Uncle, I am sure it's not the Bihari boy.'

'Raseel, Robert is saying he tried his best to keep you out of it. I didn't hear what you told the police officer but…'

'Uncle, I just have to tell the cop what I saw, what I think. This has nothing to do with Robert.'

What on earth had I got myself into? Was this the summer of madness that Aila and I had planned over telephonic giggles? Innocent plans to relive our childhood strolls through pine-scented forests and along quiet lakes full of secrets, to rest our eyes on emerald hills that roll on and on in the distance to touch a sapphire sky. Maybe we focused too much on the word 'madness' and that was exactly what was happening.

17

'The cop has left,' the man said, switching off his mobile. The man on the opposite hill, in the tall, white house with windows like tired eyes.

His companion kept looking out of the window, unmoved, puffing furiously. Finally he spoke.

'Did she…?'

'Yes, she did. She said she saw three guys in the cottage. First they left and then the dkhar left. She also told the cop that one of the men had leucoderma.'

'Get Ribok on the line. He has to leave immediately. It will be tough in this weather but he will have to manage.'

'He will. Kong Rivulet returned a few days ago. She said it was tough especially because of the leeches but she…'

'Still managed and brought a lot of "maal". I admire that woman. I hope she has brought some jackets.'

'Is that all you want?'

'Yeah, at this moment. Did you get Ribok?'

The youngest of the three in a peak cap and matching sneakers nodded. 'But he says he has fever…'

'Give me the phone. Ribok? Yeah, yeah, just carry some paracetemol and run. Once you cross the border you will be well looked after.'

This was the same border that thousands of East Bengalis crossed over to India during the Partition in 1947 and many, out of choice, even before that. Here, in these hills in a world so different from where they came, bewildered and insecure, they could not integrate. Marwaris had come earlier, soon after the British had conquered Assam in 1826. They monopolized trade for there was no competition at that time. Meghalaya was carved out of Assam and formed on 21 January 1972. The Marwaris, along with the Sindhis, held control of commerce and trade well into the 1970s. The Bengalis manned the offices, banks, and the grocery and photography shops. The resentment of the locals, especially the men, was palpable. They stood convinced that the dkhars were the enemies of the land, the grabbers and usurpers of what could have been theirs. At the same time they knew that that was only half the story.

The other half festered in their minds.

18

I felt relieved and completely exhausted after the cop left. The sun suddenly disappeared and clouds gathered in the sky. For a long time I didn't speak to Uncle Rangshan who sat quietly by my side as Aila's brothers and various relations and friends were engrossed in whispered discussions.

A strong smell of rain wafted into the room and the whispers stopped. Everyone sat hunched and silent like old monks in prayer, decoding the messages of the turbulent sky. In the distance the thunder rumbled and flashes of lightning, sharp, swift, sword-like, lit up the sky while the rain poured steadily, regally, undeterred.

'Raseel, you should have called me up immediately when you saw those boys.'

'I didn't think there was anything unusual, uncle,' I lied.

'I suppose so…but I wish you had mentioned it to Kmie U Flin or even Robert.'

I kept quiet.

How much can one lie?

Uncle Rangshan looked so concerned. I knew he was as worried for me as he was for Aila and Aibor. I put my head on his shoulder and closed my eyes.

19

In a room inside the tall house with windows like tired, hollow eyes, the phone rang.

All at once the atmosphere altered, the tension was palpable. Another day had passed. It was the midnight of the day after. Strong and Ksan looked fatigued but charged.

'I know there was no audience this time,' Strong said gruffly into the phone. 'How many houses? Ok, hmm... come right away. No, just walk, walk through the locality lanes, and pretend you are drunk. Two of you can do that. Talk about a Hindi film, hum a tune. That will throw the CRP guys totally off scent. Come.'

'Why tonight? Strong, they could have...'

'No, no. I want them to report eye to eye. They should always report this way. Just hearing is not enough. I want to see these boys, their body language, their tone, their eyes. They have to see ME. I have to make them burn inside like we used to... like WE used to.'

'Shit! Yeah, like we used to.'

Strong grunted and pulling the bottle of whiskey out of the cabinet, poured himself a drink.

'It's a bit early isn't it?'

'Stop it, Ksan. What's early and what's late? I am so tired, I am so goddamned tired.'

'That's exactly what I am saying. Just relax for a while.'

'I am so tired of it all, Ksan, not just this moment. I am tired of all this shit,' Strong shouted. 'Where is all this going to lead? We are just following the Boss' orders. It's been going on for so long.'

'He thinks, plans, orders and…'

'And we follow, right? Yet does that scum care? Will all this really bring the government to the table? Does the government care? Does Delhi care? Does anyone care? Or are we being used, just simply being used for the Boss' gains? He is using us, Ksan. He is using these kids too. They are doing what they believe is going to eventually lead them to a better future—jobs, opportunities, a great life ahead. Poor things!'

'Like we did once…'

'Yes.'

'And look at us now, mere castrated bulls.'

'Shut up, Strong.'

'I won't.' Strong poured himself another drink and gulped it down. His eyes were closed; his hands were clenched as his heart burnt inside.

'Come on, Strong. We may be wrong.'

'Shut up, Ksan, just SHUT UP.'

'Strong, go home and just relax for a while.'

'Home? Hah! That hell—that is where all the trouble starts. Yesterday I told my wife that her mother was a fat sow and you know what she did? She walked off in a huff in the middle of the night and went and slept in that very sow's room, in her bed.'

'Well, I don't think it was right of you to call your kiaw a fat sow.'

'Oh no? Oh YES, Ksan, yes! That old hag had the guts to tell me to throw away the orange peels!'

'So what? She's an elder.'

'Don't butt in, LISTEN. That bastard, Kenstar, my

youngest sister-in-law's husband, was the culprit. He was sitting on the steps, peeling orange after orange and throwing them around. He was sitting there eating oranges, spitting the seeds from his filthy mouth—just like that, and I am supposed to…'

'Strong, that's bad.'

'Yes and you also know why I am subjected to such treatment. I am not the khatduh's husband, I am not a government officer like that bloody slop, I can't move my wife and kids out from the family home so this is what I get. THIS is what I GET.'

'Just move out, Strong. If your wife can't stand by you, just move out.'

'And go—where?'

'Back to your mother's house. That is the custom.'

'Think then speak, Ksan. Think and then speak. Mei also has my youngest sister with her, my father's pet and who is HER husband, my so very smart friend?'

'Oh yes! I didn't think of that.'

'Yeah, the cop. On top of that he suspects me. I think he does. So far he doesn't want to do anything about it.'

'Batriti is a good girl. She won't let you down.'

'So where do we go tonight? After the kids are gone? How about that girl from Malki? She seemed pretty keen, huh?

'Which one?'

'Well, the one I thought looked like Michelle Yeoh.'

'Oh, yes, but what clan is she?'

'Ksan! For God's sake.'

'Yes, for God's sake.'

'I don't care.'

'You do, so do I, so does everyone else. You can't go around sleeping with a clanswoman.'

'Damn.'

20

Two of Aila's aunts and their daughters moved in that same evening. Aila's brother moved in too with two other men who worked for him. Kmie U Flin buzzed around the house to make them comfortable. She readied the rooms and with the help of Titi and a maid of one of the aunts, whipped up a delicious dinner. Lunch had been brought from outside by one of the relatives. Kmie U Flin would break into sobs every now and then, remembering the two missing boys. Everyone was upset that a crime had been committed in such a respectable house. Kmie U Flin was distraught because 'Sures and Rabi' had disappeared.

That made two of us, just two of us.

21

'Whatever it is, Strong, for the sake of your mother and sister we can't mess up our lives further…and for the sake of your children…'

'Don't mention them, Ksan. Don't! Not my kids! Shit, I'm so fucking mad…'

'Stop it, Strong.'

But it was too late. Strong had whipped out a pen knife and slashed it across his palm.

'I want to erase these lines. This awful fate.'

'Strong…'

The blood started to drip. Ksan had never seen such gall, such sadness emanating from his childhood friend. He started to shiver, feeling as if the entire universe was crumbling around him like old, worm-eaten walls.

Just then there was a knock on the door. Three young men entered. They saw the blood. They said nothing.

'Sit down, tell us,' Ksan whispered.

'How many houses?'

'Three.'

'Did that khar suh nep, the rajaiwala, flee? I mean, was it done as it should have been done?'

'Yes. As soon as we started on him his neighbour…'

'Kong Deng?'

'Yes, she came out and did her bit, she saved him as planned.'

'That's good. He is a Mussalman…'

'Yes, we understand. Bah Ribok is on his way…he has

reached Dawki. About to cross the border when I last spoke to him.'

'Good! On his way to safety and comfort, to the khar suh nep's country. Yes, that's the deal, kid.Ok, you may all leave now. We'll let you know…' Ksan said.

'Thanks, boys. Well done,' Strong slurred and slumped back on the sofa.

The phone rang. Strong stretched his arm and picked it up.

'No,' he said. 'We have to stop the cops from going to Bihar. If they catch that fellow Rabi, we'll be in trouble. He left for Gorakhpur, didn't he? Stop him at all cost.'

22

Next morning I woke up early and switched on Radio Shillong. I lay in bed for a while listening to the melodious Khasi songs sung by the beautiful Kong Helen Giri. The music transported me to a faraway land where Man and Nature merged in perfect melody. I didn't hear Titi coming in. She put the tray down and told me that Ravi had been caught and had confessed to the crime. She was hysterical. Her eyes were large pools of fear, her face ashen. She thrust the paper at me. My head spun as I read,'The murder of a Bihari employee of a private residence in Lawbah colony has been solved with the arrest of the victim's cousin, Ravi Rai, who has confessed to the crime, police sources confirmed today. The body of the victim is not yet traced but the police are confident that the crime will be solved expediently after this breakthrough.'

The newspaper slid to the floor as I stared at the rain pouring from a grey impassive sky. It beat angrily on the tin roof that spread over the large hill bungalow and the residents who had suddenly been aroused from their peaceful existence by a hitherto unknown, unimaginable incident. The rain continued its drumming on the tin roof. At least Nature commiserated with me and I felt somewhat at peace as my tea lay in front of me on a cane tray made in Tripura. I closed my eyes and imagined that my weary head rested on the shoulder of the mountain slope framed by my window. *'I live not in myself but I become/ Portion of that around me; and to me/ High mountains are a feeling.'* I felt the tears stinging my eyes and I slipped into a second sleep, lulled by the words of an almost forgotten poem. When I woke up the skies had cleared, so typically Shillong. It was noon.

'Robert, I'd like to go for a drive.'

'Where, Kong?'

'Anywhere.'

'Why don't you visit someone? You will feel better. Kong Aila and Bah Aibor are probably arriving day after tomorrow.'

'Let us go to town and beyond…towards Nongthymmai. I will visit Sngithiang. You remember, no?'

'Yes, but they no longer stay there. They are now on the road behind the Raj Bhavan on the way to the golf course. Her father is a minister.'

'Really, so let us go there. It is even closer.'

Sngithiang—Sweet Sun—was in school with Aila and me. She did her graduation from Shillong and also married her childhood boyfriend, Paul. She produced four kids and was blissfully married for twelve or thirteen years until his bouts of drinking turned into alcoholism. It hurt Sngithiang deeply and she began to suffer from depression. Paul did not die of cirrhosis as many did in Shillong but one Sunday afternoon he slipped down Sngithiang's polished stairway and broke his neck. Aila told me that for many months Nini was inconsolable. She blamed her anti-depressant drugs for preventing her from waiting for her husband's lunch at 4 p.m.—'after all it was Sunday'. She blamed Jackie Chan for keeping her children glued to the TV instead of escorting their inebriated father to the toilet, her parents for sleeping after lunch like plainsmen and her servants for going to church. I was sad and shaken to get the news of Paul's fatal accident. Nini was one friend who wrote long letters and extolled the virtues of marriage—the exquisite feeling of complete fulfillment when she bathed, powdered and dressed each child, laid out their meals and watched them eat while she fed the youngest one, the joy of taking them out for drives and watching them play amidst the pines and pick wild daisies in the meadows below Shillong Peak while she and Paul held hands, totally content. Dipsomania was a genetic problem in Paul's family, or so it seemed. All his three maternal uncles died of excessive drinking.

As the car climbed up the slope, out of the wrought iron gate onto the main road, I felt my body loosening up. I leaned back and relaxed and told Robert to play an Elvis Presley cassette. I let my eyes feast on all the sights that they could take in—houses fronted with pots of geraniums blooming along with gerberas, daisies, pansies and orchids, their hues and shades dancing in the late morning sun. Was day before yesterday a dream?

The Sanskrit name Meghalaya, 'the Abode of the Clouds', was suggested by the linguist, Dr Suniti Kumar Chatterjee, who was doing a study in these hills between 1926 and 1932. Dr Chatterjee was, apparently, overwhelmed by the masses and masses of clouds that hung from the sky for days on end. The suggestion was taken up in 1972 when the Khasis, Jaintias and Garos separated from Assam and attained statehood and Shillong become the capital. By then I was in faraway Delhi but I joined the celebrations at an IAS officer's residence in RK Puram where many of the Meghalayans had gathered to toast their new State. I hugged each one like a long-lost friend and insisted on getting high on Honey Bee Brandy, avoiding all the Scotches, wines and pricey liqueurs.

Once the car dipped into the lower part of town, the small pretty cottages gave way to cantonment buildings, official-looking but bearable, and then to the ultimate depressants, ill-kept government establishments that resembled old cardboard cartons put hurriedly together. I closed my eyes and listened to Elvis singing, *'Well they're so lonely baby/ They'll be so lonely, they could die.'*

'Robert,' I said, leaning forward, putting my chin on the back of the front seat, where I should have been sitting if I wasn't so confused and so completely out of sorts.

'Yes, Kong?'

'Robert, you know who killed Suresh, don't you?'

The answer had no voice because it didn't need one.

23

'So how is it going?' she asked, lowering the volume of the television, her breasts almost spilling out of her new night gown.

He winced and wished he hadn't splurged on the lingerie on his last visit to New Delhi. He had to, however, because he was trying hard to impress the boutique owner, the girlfriend of a real estate don, whose voluptuousness was, to him, unparalleled. At the party, later on that evening, she let him hold her close. He had spent fifty thousand rupees in her boutique. And why not? The deal had just been signed and his wallet felt heavy—and his heart too, for some strange reason.

'Can't say in these matters,' he replied wistfully, thinking of the Delhi boobs as he started undressing. 'Even if I become CM how do I solve the problem?'

'How does it matter? We'll enjoy ourselves for a few years…'

'Yeah?'

'Ok, months. At least they'll say he was a chief minister once. God is great. I could never imagine this day would come. Imagine, I almost married Winston. Imagine! He is still where he is—a village school teacher.'

'That's life. Winston, with a name like that, is still where he is and me—Justice is on the verge of reaching the top…most unjustly.'

'What, Jus?' she asked, already absorbed once again in the delights of television, the joke lost on her.

He went back to the drawing room and dialled a number. He thanked God for giving him a dim and scatty woman. There was never anything to worry about.

24

The traffic increased. We slowed down. We were, by then, parallel to the Garrison Ground where we used to have the Annual Sports Day. The Civil Hospital had acquired a brighter face, the State Central Library retained its sombre look and looked quite awkward opposite the elegant Church of England with its so very English face. I observed all that but in my heart my question stood waiting for Robert's answer which did not come. Robert was like that. No one could ever shove him around. He had his own pace. Aibor was the more easy one, always cheerful and relaxed. I started missing Aibor and Aila terribly as the car took a turn.

The Meghalaya Secretariat flashed past in pink and grey and then came Rap's Mansion and the DC's court, both bustling for different reasons. Soon Ward's Lake came into view and my eyes misted over. I gazed at the lake; a few boats lounged languidly on one side for the holiday season was over. Scattered on the slopes was, to me, an unfamiliar sight, groups of scruffy boys lazing, kind of incongruous, but what the hell, it was their land and if they wanted to pretty up the landscape—fine.

I asked Robert to park on the side. I looked at the lake for a long, long time. There used to be two or three suicides every year, mainly lovers. I suppose that was the time when love was worth dying for. At that moment I was thinking of Kmie U Flin's love for the two boys, her 'Sures and Rabi'. I felt good just knowing that goodness still existed.

'Robert, you know who killed Suresh, don't you? Who is it, Robert?'

'I did...as much as you did.'

'I want to meet Ravi, Robert.'

But even as I blurted out those words, I knew the timing was wrong.

25

'Ribok has crossed the border.'

'Good.'

'Badly bitten by mosquitoes, leeches he warded off with tobacco and salt, yeah, he wore long, tight socks.'

'Was he alone?'

'No, Kong Jlah and her gang were there. They had gone for their maal.'

'Any reaction from the woman from Delhi about the arrest?'

'No, not so far.'

'Good. Keep tab anyway.'

'When is she leaving?

'She has to meet Kong Aila…'

'Does she?' The question hissed through the air and hung around unanswered.

Strong sipped his beer for it was hot and humid.

Ksan slumped into a chair and lit a cigarette.

26

I kept staring at the lake, waiting for Robert to say something, knowing very well that it wasn't going to come so easy. My eyes climbed up the slope to the Shillong Club established by British planters and officers in the early part of the twentieth century. It was a beautiful club with a green roof and wooden rooms. That was the club where we all used to go and dance, Aila and me and our friends, whenever the Mess didn't have a party and my family could escape the Army crowd and meet the local gentry. Often we would walk down to the lake and stroll along its moon-washed waters. Those were days when even holding hands in stolen moments was the height of delicious promiscuity. The lake was dug and constructed under the supervision of a Colonel Hopkins and eventually named after the Chief Commissioner of Assam, Sir William Ward. The local people call it Nan Polok (Nan's lake) after the convict who did most of the digging, or so I was told.

'The old club was so beautiful. Remember, Robert?'

'It burnt down.'

'I know but they could have replaced it with something better than this scowling, cement monstrosity.'

'There's ugliness everywhere,' he said as the road curled down coquettishly to the Polo Ground and onto the Golf Links.

My heart began to beat. I was getting somewhere. Somewhere as far as Robert was concerned, somewhere too to a place, a part of the universe I loved and cherished. The eighteen-hole golf course, situated at 4,750 feet above sea level, was reputedly the highest in the world, a chunk of emerald spread out with pine trees all around. But when I reached there my heart sank. There was barbed wire fencing on one side, houses had mushroomed all along the parallel road and people strolled around casually on the links as if it was a forgotten park.

'Robert, you know who killed Suresh, don't you?' I asked again.

Silence, silence and more silence.

'Don't you think you should tell the police?'

'No.'

'No? Why?'

'It has nothing to do with the police.'

'A murder has been committed and you think it has nothing to do with the police?'

'Yes, it has nothing to do with the police, it's not a crime.'

'Do you know what a crime is, Robert?

'A forbidden act punishable by law—according to the dictionary.'

'So?'

'So?'

'Robert…'

'See, words and definitions in the dictionary apply to normal life. Let's say there are others who have a different dictionary.'

'Oh! And in their dictionary this is not a crime, huh!'

'No. Crime is not understanding another person's pain, not having the courage to accept the cause of that person's pain, not doing anything about it. That is a crime.'

'And you think Suresh and his lot are the representatives of the criminals?'

'No, Kong, no. Didn't I say earlier that they are the punching bags?'

We were sitting on a slope in the Golf Course sharing a packed brunch of Richmond ham sandwiches and garden-fresh lettuce. With my stomach just nicely full, my heart brimmed over with confidence as usual and I, therefore, dared to take one of Minna Jaiswal's numerous pieces of advice—take on life, face it head on and never be evasive. The more one hid the more one would be found.

'Kong,' it was almost a whisper. 'There is a war going on, a silent war, the rules are different.'

'A disgusting war, Robert, a coward's war. Taking it out on innocent people. How could you be part of it?' I was shouting.

'It's just a different kind of war, Kong. Yes, the act committed is merely a statement. Unless something like this happens nobody bothers,' he persisted, still in whispers. It was scary but I was not going to let that stop me.

'Robert, you are odious,' I, too, lowered my voice to a whisper. Shouting is a sign of weakness.

'We don't expect people, all the people to understand. How can you all when...when our mothers don't?'

'Robert, there has to be a better way out—there HAS to be. Why don't you all just change to a patrilineal society?'

'WHAT? Can you just one fine day decide to be matrilineal? Each one of us belong to a kur, a clan which is as important as your gotra. But yes, there should, at least, be equality as far as inheritance and so on goes. After all, how does one function without money, goddammit! But nobody wants to disturb the status quo, nobody wants to be flung into a state of discomfort. Comfort is happiness isn't it, Kong? They would do anything for it. Anything!'

'Yes, Robert, this time I cannot refute your statement. People sell themselves, their wives, their children to be comfortable. They do equate comfort with happiness. They would do anything for it. Faraway in a city in the north a beautiful aunt of mine had to sleep with a hideous judge. Thereafter her husband won an important land case. Everybody was comfortable…and happy after that.'

'So, Kong, like you have understood that, one day, you will understand this too, inshallah.'

'What? Did I hear you say…'

'Yes, inshallah. I like this word. I learnt it from my Muslim friends. Two of them and their families have converted to Islam. Their fathers are dkhars from Bangladesh.'

'Really?'

'Yes, so many others too. That is yet another story.'

'Robert, let us just stick to one story now. When you

are ready, please tell me who killed Suresh and why and also why are you protecting the killer or killers. You have answered in riddles but I want it in black and white. I saw a murder being committed, Robert, and I just cannot keep quiet like this. Please understand. You will tell me won't you, Robert?'

'Inshallah,' and he walked towards the car and got in.

27

'Bah, we have done everything now—killed, burnt, lied, cheated, what next?'

'Think, boys, think this CM has to go. Then we'll move.' Roland Lamare adjusted his tie and put his hands inside the pockets of his dark grey trousers, part of his get-up for the day. The blue blazer was a Pierre Cardin, which his son-in-law, a doctor in England, had presented him for Christmas. He looked more like a well-preserved glamour boy rather than a high-profile ex-politician as he paced up and down the room.

'Let's expose his philandering,' roared Strong, sipping his whiskey.

'Yes, he has a love child from a young girl living somewhere in Upper Shillong.'

'So?' Roland Lamare suddenly turned, hands still in pockets, as if he was on the ramp modelling his vanity. 'There are love children everywhere. Legitimacy is every child's birthright. That is the law of the land since time immemorial.'

'Yes, but not from a woman from the wrong clan?'

'Huh?'

'Yeah.'

'She's a…?'

'No, but apparently her clan and his are forbidden to marry. She comes from a sub-clan. I forget the name.'

'Ah! Then that's it, boys,' Lamare chuckled and lit an India King. When Jus Lyngdoh becomes the CM, he would light a Davidoff, he thought to himself.

A quiet sob suddenly intruded into the buoyant atmosphere from the corner of the room, where the volunteers were seated.

'What's wrong, kid?' Strong thundered, as Lamare's eyes narrowed and his eyebrows knotted with concern.

'The girl... The girl is my sister. Please don't publicize it, please, please, I beg of you. Our family will be disgraced forever.'

'Do you care more about your family or the Cause?'

The boy continued to sob, his sobs getting louder and louder, despair in every note, while the discussion continued, unabated.

'Answer me,' thundered Strong. The boy kept sobbing.

'See, son, once you join the Movement you have to think only for its good. That is very important. We will obviously compensate you handsomely for your sacrifice,' Roland Lamare said, the words falling easily, like water from a tap.

Ksan went to the toilet, sat on the WC and sobbed.

28

It felt strange and exhilarating to be soaking in the gentle light of a Shillong evening, breathing pine-scented air, thinking of the past and coping with the present. Two different worlds, so far apart, never to meet. The past so different it seemed a separate lifetime almost.

Then suddenly Robert spoke, 'My father left Mei for a younger woman. We all felt embarrassed, abandoned and insecure. My brother started smoking hash and he also drank. It was terrible when he drank, he was so aggressive I had to, sometimes, hit him and protect Mei, it was terrible, it really was.'

Either Robert did not know who his real father was or he was hiding the fact from me. I didn't want to touch the subject—such an irrelevant subject.

'How did your mother cope?'

'She just carried on. Not a word of remorse or protest. She had a tea stall in the market very close to Pine Grove School. She did good business with all the ayahs and drivers who used to come and pick up the children. Some teachers had a daily order with her for their lunch. She was so good with her tea and snacks that one of the Pine Grove parents who was establishing a nursing home asked her to move and manage the canteen. She did it and that gave a big boost to our finances. My brother and I assisted Mei most enthusiastically. We prospered; we bought a new fridge, a colour TV, a fancy cassette player. My mother realized one of her dreams and admitted my sister to one of the better English medium schools in Malki. All three of us could have studied in a school for the price of that one school. Imagine! We should have told Mei and protested but it didn't cross our minds. We didn't think of it. Our brains were so fried up, so bloody fried up.'

I knew I was getting somewhere and I kept quiet, waiting for him to continue.

'With this newfound comfort, my brother recovered, kicked his drug habits and did his Matric privately. He's now a primary school teacher in Mawphlang. Remember Mawphlang, Kong?'

'Yes, Captain Hunt's cherry brandy and the fascinating Sacred Groves. How could I forget?'

'Well, life went on. I used to feel pangs of pain whenever I dropped Christine to school but I kept it to myself. I was young and, as I said, as boys, we didn't expect to get the best or whatever. Then, one day, it was Christmas Eve and Mei was working extra hard on some special orders and my sister was in her room laughing and chatting with her friends, trying on her new dresses. As I was looking at my present, a 1000-rupee watch, Mei asked me to come and help her in the kitchen. Something inside me snapped. I walked into the kitchen and broke everything I could lay my hands on. Next morning Bah Aibor's parents came and took me away. They bought a taxi for me and I began to drive and earn. I liked it but, honestly, it was too much of a rough and tough job for me. My aunt, Bah Aibor's mother, realized this and before I could break more things she requested me to accompany Aibor and live with him in his new house—Kong Aila's. She is the youngest daughter so he had to move to her house. They are all wonderful people. They asked me to choose what kind of work I wanted to do. Well, now I manage all their affairs—the home, the vehicles, the accounting of all the various businesses along with the official accountants, I drive. I like driving most of all, I am comfortable but it doesn't solve the problem, Kong, it doesn't.'

'I am afraid I don't understand, Robert.'

'There are a few intelligent, thinking guys who have started a movement to change the system to tell people here to value their sons. Nobody listens.'

He was quiet for a while and then he said, 'Poor Suresh. Such a good kid. Kong, we must save Ravi. It wasn't him.'

29

'The exposure will take a few days. Let's find all the details and do a proper job...where did he meet her, how did it happen, how old is the child. Fathering a child of a clanswoman...crazy!'

'Sub clan. That was how he goofed. Yes, before that let us give another shot. We cannot be silent. Nothing will be solved.'

'We've already organized that.'

'Great,' grunted Strong and lit a cigar.

'I am glad you are in a good mood,' Ksan commented.

'Aah! Of course I am. I had a great night with Allie.'

'Allie who?'

'I don't know and who cares, the Boss arranged it all for me.'

'We should not have chosen Bah Aibor's house.'

'The Boss wanted it. He was sure about it. He wanted the incident to take place in a high-profile home so that the crime could get noticed. He was very clear that he wanted it to look like a breakdown of law and order problem, not just ethnic cleansing. A double-barrelled shot. Everyone will then go for Bah Jus. Remember he has a huge outsider vote bank as well. The Boss plans well, huh!'

'Not very clever were we, to let the other boy go?'

'Didn't want to kill two. No need. No, he won't sneak. He wouldn't want his whole family sent to hell, would he, by sneaking? Relax. It had to be done and you know why.'

'I don't know, Strong, I don't know. I can't get over the last meeting. That was too much. Just too much.'

'It had to be done...the killing had to be done. We can't have traitors. We had to show the rest that it can happen to them. We had to convey this to everyone. Rich or poor, big or small. We can't have deserters and police informers getting away!'

'How is all this helping, I don't understand. The guys up there—the rich and privileged—are not bothered at all. Their children get on, anyway. Their futures are secure. Their education—the best possible—is assured and meticulously planned by their parents. They are, believe me, totally unaware of the problems here. A nephew of mine studying in Pune, asked what the fuss was all about. Before I could reply, a niece studying in Delhi snapped, 'I swear, what's the fuss all about? Such a nuisance, these stupid bandhs.' They were not really interested to know. This little incident was an eye opener.'

Strong gritted his teeth and his eyes narrowed. 'Till we find an answer, let us kill some, burn some, cheat some. Oh, yeah, let us let us...'

'Strong, stop it, don't make it worse. DON'T!'

'I won't, I won't. I can still recall those secret meetings in the Boss' house. We were planning the strategy for our demands for our own university and a law college. We genuinely thought it was the highway to the stars. We were so thrilled sitting with the Boss in that drawing room of his, drinking good whiskey, feeling sophisticated and committed. He was the first rebel who made us aware, who started the whole movement, a king-maker, someone who could talk straight to the dkhars. We worshipped him. We did! We thought he was great, he was God, he was the Saviour who has come into our miserable, rudderless lives

to help us realize our dreams and lead us to a bright future. We didn't know, innocent young idiots that we were, that he was merely recruiting us as his private army, which he could use to further his own dream and political career. I feel strange saying all this, Ksan, I am not feeling good hearing myself speaking the truth, but I have to. It has to come out.'

'Yeah, I guess so.'

'Imagine, we actually thought he was a good and selfless man, our saviour who has given up his political career to liberate us. Imagine! Two decades have passed, Ksan, twenty summers with the length of two long winters. Look at our protruding bellies and thinning hair.'

'Yes, yes…'

'Don't look so resigned, Ksan. Look inside your screwed up mind and heart and spirit. What is left of you and me? We are just pitiable insects which he drags out when he needs to. Strike, little serpents. Strike, strike, strike. Then when his objective is achieved he herds us back into our little cells.'

'Strong, this generation is cleverer. They won't let the likes of him drag them around. Not for too long. He will have to perform.'

'Hah! That's what you think! He will get his way. He always does. "Lots of money coming in, boys. So what's the problem? Just be more generous with your time, your head and your heart"…and Ksan, it just takes two notes to cover your eyes. He knew, the bastard knew that and now he controls everyone in the state—ministers, bureaucrats, cops, businessmen and us and everyone, everyone. That scum controls the destiny of our land. Oh Ksan…'

'Strong, let us do something. Let us plan something, a better strategy. Let us dream a better dream…something more beneficial. Let us benefit from something somewhere. We can't let the kids be fooled like this. We have to tell them, guide them. I feel terrible.'

'What new strategy, huh? Just advise them to make sure that the Boss and the smaller bosses stick by them. Otherwise once they become ministers and have used these kids and sucked votes out of wide-eyed hapless victims like vampires going voo voo voo in their vehicles, red lights flashing, they will very gently push these kids out. So gently they won't even know. Look at us, did we ever imagine in our wildest dreams that we will remain like this? What should we call ourselves? Pathetic assholes also have a name, you know! Say something, Ksan.'

'Ok, so we are the Boss' stooges, so what? We have not reached the top but our conscience is clear. We have not lied to anyone. We have not cheated the public. We simply followed orders.'

'We have not cheated anyone? Our hands are soiled with the blood of innocents and you are saying we have not cheated and lied?'

'It's a war, Strong. In a war the blood of innocents flows but we never promised the youth any sort of paradise. There are no broken promises.'

'Ksan, you really surprise me. We damn well promised by carrying out all those orders of the Boss who is forever giving speeches filled with promises. All to fulfill the dreams of his own coterie. Scum!'

'Stop it, Strong. I know. I know. I was just trying not to know.'

'Ksan, all I can see are the red lights flashing, cheery grins, friendly waves. We are your saviours we will protect your lands and your jobs from being grabbed, your women being taken away, your spirits being crushed. Inside their minds are blank, their souls are jammed, they care a damn. Tell me what is the difference between them and the earlier rulers—the British, the Assamese, the Indians? Eventually it is just about the powerful versus the powerless.'

'The dkhars—yes, they always look down on us.'

'Ah, do not make that mistake, Ksan. The Boss and company do not look up to us either! They no longer consider us equals. Once all the outsiders have fled, got rid of under this false pretence, when these starry-eyed kids start to wonder, when they can no longer drown their confusion and fears in drinks, drugs and sex, then whose blood will flow in this bloody rampage? Whose blood Ksan, whose blood?'

'Don't, Strong. Stop it. You are talking like a mad man.'

'All those dearly paid for hopes will have to be appeased. The insatiable demons of greed, power and money will have to be appeased. They have released the virus. They have created their own Armageddon. They will plunder their own land and destroy their own people. Khasi will destroy Khasi. The process has already begun. They will be blind to everything but money and power.'

Ksan looked at his friend. Speechless. He knew he was right.

The phone rang. Ksan picked it up and for some reason closed his eyes tight.

'Strong, the Boss wants us to meet him near the lake. First bridge—he will be in a white Maruti.'

'Asshole.'

30

As we drove in through the gate and down the slope, I could see the house crouching like a huge, slumbering dinosaur. Tall pines stood sentinel on either side and hydrangeas of mauve and pink sat eloquently on the gentle slopes. It was the season of rain and mists and spectacular sunsets.

I saw, as the car purred down to the porch, that the gardener's cottage had its lights on.

'Robert, there's someone in the cottage. Look, lights!'

'Hmm…' he muttered casually but his head turned immediately to look towards the cottage.

'I am going down to see. How long can I pretend that nothing is happening and stay out of this?'

He followed me. I could feel his sullenness with each footstep. Then I saw Kmie U Flin, waddling out of the front door with two other women. One was a middle-aged woman who was neatly dressed in a grey and blue jainsem. My eyes quickly took in the grey flowers on the navy blue background and the matching blue merina tapmohkhlieh covering her head. Long gold earrings with blue glass drops brushed against her neck and on her feet, she wore a pair of neat black sandals with low heels. She reminded me so much of Christina, my favourite Khasi maid, and my eyes smarted as my spirits lifted a little. The third person was Titi.

The voices grew louder as they got closer. Kmie U Flin's voice was clear and excited.

'Keep the mud from the front of the house in the small bag and the one from the back in the bigger one so that we will be able to identify. Careful, careful, don't slip. Titi, are you sure you took the mud from the foot of the front steps? That's where the killers must have definitely stepped. Oh ho! How could this happen? Poor Rabi! Poor Sures! Waw ko mei!' Kmie U Flin burst into tears. Then the other voice took over.

'Be brave, Pli. We will definitely get the killers. I have told Bah To that we would like to consult the Mussalman as well. I believe he is very powerful and also accurate in his readings. We will get to the bottom of this, don't worry.'

I stepped out from behind the azaleas and light-heartedly made a face to scare them. They started laughing, Titi giggled. They seemed grateful for the small reprieve.

'Kong Raseel this is Kong Bonili. She has come to help us solve the murder,' said Titi excitedly.

'Khublei, Kong Bonili. It's so kind of you to come and be with us…but, actually one is not supposed to be roaming in the scene of the crime. The cops will get angry, Kmie U Flin.'

'We are not just roaming around, Kong Raseel.We are also going to try and find out who has committed this crime.' She said it all in one breath with a twinkle in her eye and an uncharacteristic firmness in her tone. All that before she burst into tears again as Kong Bonili gathered her protectively in her arms.

'Now, now, stop crying, Pli. We are going to catch the killers. Bah To has never failed. Never.'

'Bah To?' I was surprised. 'Who is he, a private detective? If he is, he should be here himself.'

'Bah To is a nongpeit. He will tell us exactly what happened. He will know everything from the mud we are carrying, their towels and the hair the boys have left behind in their combs. Well, one of them has.'

'You broke into the cottage?' I was horrified.

'Indeed not but there is one window they did not seal...'

I gave up as Titi burst into nervous giggles once again.

'Well, all right but how is the hair going to help Bah To?'

It soon became clear that the two women were going to seek the assistance of a nongpeit, a tantric soothsayer. He would check the mud and the hair they had brought and then with eggs, roosters and rice unravel the mystery and then advise further.

'Please let me come with you. When are you going?' I pleaded.

I had heard of crystal gazers in London and similar soothsayers all over India.

'We are leaving the house at 6 a.m., come what may.'Again that determined tone surfaced in the old lady's voice.

'I'll be up at five. I'll make my own tea. In fact, I will make tea for everyone.'

'No, no. I'll be up. I'll do that and I also need a cup of tea right now.'

I was feeling rather excited walking beside the two

ladies who were chattering in Khasi about esoteric remedies.

Then as we entered the kitchen and settled down Robert staggered in. I stared at his face and I could feel the blood slowly draining from my face. His eyes were bloodshot with ire and despair. My hand stretched out towards him. He shrank.

'Kong Raseel, you want to go and hunt down the murderers? Don't waste time. How many will you hunt down? They are everywhere, in each one of us. Once you think of something it takes life, everything begins from thought. The very thought is the act.'

31

The grey waters of the man-made lake lay placidly under a heavy monsoon sky. The hills around gleamed with the freshness of a just-gone shower and the trees were still shaking off the drops. On one side of the iron bridge that spanned a gaping gorge a white Maruti van was parked. Very soon an old Willys jeep came bouncing down the hill road with a trailer full of loaded sacks. Freshly made brooms stuck out from all sides of the worn-out trailer. Two young men, one at the wheel and one in the front seat chewed kwai purposefully. Their eyes moved as they scoured the hillsides, the river beds, the scattered clumps of trees. The driver looked into the mirror, settled it just right and as they neared the stationary Maruti, he slowed down and then stopped.

'Everything all right?' he shouted loud and clear, quite unnecessarily so.

A head stuck out.

'No, something is wrong with the car. Can you help out?'

The driver of the jeep got down and slid into the front seat of the car, next to the driver. His companion walked to the bridge and lit a cigarette, all the time scouring the countryside through small, slit eyes. The driver of the jeep then got down and opened the bonnet of the car, tinkered for a while and got into the car again. In the back seat two men in dark glasses sat, middle-aged with receding hairlines and bulbous booze-red noses, their lips crimson with paan stains and a hundred lies.

Fifteen, twenty minutes passed, then the young man slid out to the car.

'I think it should be all right now.'

The man walked to his jeep. His companion joined him from the bridge as the landscape darkened and the clouds looked ready to drop.

The Maruti van sped away along the dam. It went as far as the village of Sumer. Once the road dipped into a lonely stretch, the car reversed and took the road back to Shillong. The jeep was not far behind but, instead of continuing straight down towards Sumer it turned left where the dam ended. The road it took had luxury farm houses dotting the landscape on one side and the freshly cut hillside on the other, gaping red like unwashed meat.

The jeep stopped a little beyond the stretch. The two young men unloaded the sacks and let them roll down the forested slopes. The sacks burst open as small stones tumbled out in showers to disappear into the tall grass. The two men sat in silence, smoking, as they stared ahead at the emerald hills silhouetted against the sky, now changing colour with the falling light. A single star flickered, like a solitaire, flickering alone, sure of its dominance.

'Ksan, the Boss conveyed two things. August 15 is approaching so we have to step up our activities. He has given half the money. He couldn't siphon too much money from the canning factory project.'

'How come?'

'That nosey journalist, Irene, she brought it up in her column so the whole process has slowed down. Anyway, nothing to worry about, the funds will be pouring in. I've

got a list, here it is—the name of the minister whose house will be attacked, the number of vehicles to be burnt, the localities where we create havoc. The banners with "Khasi by birth, Indian by accident". This should be written on the walls too at strategic spots. The accent is not on communalism but breakdown of law and order. The Boss' house is also a target. He won't be there. His sentry can be disposed of if necessary.'

'Huh?'

'Obviously—it's an eyewash so that the Boss will be above suspicion. We have to see to it—ever since Irene revealed, obliquely, the possibility of his involvement during the last carnage he has to be doubly careful…'

'I don't like this name, this—the one whose house is…'

'Why?'

'Come on, he's a good guy. He works so hard for his constituency, he's not even corrupt…'

'Precisely. I think the Boss detests him for all this. In fact, that's what it is, he's the one blocking the Boss' plans to get his man where he wants, the pinnacle. And of course, there's that woman Irene who makes the dumb public suspicious with her damn articles. Anyway, first things first…'

'Did he say anything about the investigation…the Bihari boys…'

'No. He has organized everything, obviously. How could you even ask, huh? At the moment we have to focus on August 15, Independence Day. We have a major statement to make. At the meetings we have to tell the students to call for a bandh on the fourteenth and fifteenth. We have to impress upon them that this government cannot deliver and

we need a change at the top. We stick to our demands about Reservation. The Boss will see that the CM and the Cabinet do not give in. If we stretch this agitation long enough the government will fall and the Boss' guy will have a damn good chance.'

For fourteen years the state of Meghalaya had not been able to celebrate Independence Day as it was celebrated in other parts of the country. Children of that age thought August 15 was just another holiday, when schools were closed. They had never experienced flag-hoisting or sung Jana Gana Mana.

Strong lit a cigarette and inhaled deeply.

'How the hell can he influence when he is in the Opposition?'

'He has his ways. Everyone has a price, Ksan, grow up! Next the dkhars are not to be attacked.'

'Huh?'

'He said the headlines should shriek "Youth fed up with government". The rest of the work the media will do, stressing on the Reservation policy...'

'Khasi and Jaintias 60 per cent, Garos 30 per cent and others 10 per cent. Do you really think it's okay?'

'Of course. In fact we should get more. The Garos never use their seats, they can't cope. That's not important just now. Ksan, concentrate. Besides the reservation policy there's the Inner Line permit, the registration of the Bangladeshis and Nepalese at the border...'

'How the hell is he going to trust this government which is hell bent on staying on in power? The CM is determined is cling to his chair even...'

'He has his own strategy, an amazing one. He is one hell of a crook…these poor kids that he is using, if only they knew.'

'Please, Strong, don't get on that track again. Let us forget all this for a while. Look at that single star, let's make a wish.'

They had reached the top of the ridge where they could see the lights of the town glowing like a million fireflies.

'Come on, Strong, let's wish.'

'All right. I wish I was back in college again sitting under those pine trees with a girlfriend, singing. Humming. The pine needles falling softly on our heads, dreaming of becoming a government officer like my father. Dreaming of making a life with my love, a house with a white gate with a cat sunning itself on the front steps, licking its paws contentedly. I can almost see the roses and geraniums and orange trees, in the back garden, laden with fruit. I wish…I wish Pa had not left us. If he hadn't my life would have been different, Ksan, I wish I could raze the town to the ground and begin all over again.'

'What would your newfound world be like?'

'What would my newfound world be like? Well, let's see. A truly beautiful dynamic state where everyone has a job, in the villages green hills terraced with slopes of crops, trees dripping with fruit, rivers and streams teeming with fish, neat tin-roofed houses, complete families inside, healthy in mind and body. Mei serving us our favourite dish of rice and beef stew…I can taste it, Ksan, I can taste it, the cabbage boiled just right and the meat…Mei just knew how to do it right. Pa would still be with us, quiet as ever

but out of that stillness emanated all the security that we needed. God! How could he just ditch us like that—just walk from one house to another as if he was visiting. But that's what a Khasi man is, isn't he? A visitor in his wife's house. He gifts the woman his semen...'

'Stop it, Strong, that is not true. A father and his family are highly honoured in all homes. Just keep talking positive while I roll another joint, no drinking today...go on.'

'I see myself in a huge office with a circular table in front...lots of papers and pens on it, two telephones. I am a man of authority and position, suited and booted. I am doing so much for my state, my community. I live in a house with my wife and kids who respect me. Ksan, where did we go wrong?'

'You did what you thought was right, that was and is what is important...you did your best. I'll stop at the bend ahead, it's got a beautiful view of the valley...'

'I have got to pray. I've just got to. Where's the closest church?'

'So pray at the bend ahead, it's a beautiful place, it's clean, it's pure.'

'Are you crazy? I said I want to pray. Drive fast, drive to the nearest church.'

'Strong, relax, take a deep breath and pray—A Blei Trai Kynrad...'

'Ksan, don't you understand what I really want? I want my youth back, I want to live my life all over again.'

'Pray, Strong, pray.'

'For what? For the impossible?'

Then Strong sang—'Yesterday is dead and gone/ And

tomorrow's out of sight/ It's so sad to be alone/ Help me make it through the night.'

He sang softly, his head moving with the tune, his eyes swimming with the words.

Ksan started the jeep and moved into the enveloping darkness, into the night. Strong kept singing, pleading to the wind. He thought of his son, Badon, in his one-year-old grave and wished with all his heart that he was lying by his side.

32

I woke up to the sound of a true monsoon morning. The symphony of pouring rain, the colour, the fragrances, the feel entering every nook and corner of the house. Wafting past my memory like a silent ghost was the smell of the dark, musty corridors of my school, Loreto Convent, in the season of the rain. I could almost feel the warmth of the grey red-rimmed sweater underneath the blazer of darker gray emblazoned with the school crest: *Maria Regina Angelorum/Cruci Dum Spiro Fido.*

As the rain continued to pour in sheets of grey and white, I also remembered an unusual winter spent in the plains of Assam. It was December 1967. I remember it had rained like this then. The Brahmaputra crossed the danger level near a place called Dibru Darhand. We were staying in a guest house and it became so cold I had to resort to my school blazer. I had taken my school uniform along to take farewell photographs with my Assamese school friends. I had never experienced rain like that and the memory lodged within me for a long, long time.

Kmie U Flin arrived with a cup of steaming hot tea. She had made it perfectly, of course, just a hint of Darjeeling put in before straining for that special aroma. She was all set and ready to go, to brave the weather and meet the nongpeit who she was quite sure would unravel the mystery of the missing youth.

'No point in delaying as this rain won't stop for many days,' she predicted.

She was right and her firm decision prevailed in spite of strong protests from Robert and milder ones from Kong Bonili and a shivering Titi who was more scared than cold. Kmie U Flin was already dressed and ready and stepped into the rain swinging her printed made-in-China umbrella with visible determination.

We drove silently through the downpour. Robert was at his surliest best, his face ashen white. I lowered the window and the water filled my eyes, blinding me, its spray making my hair curl, its touch caressing my hand. It was as if I was in a dream. The car climbed up a steep slope beyond Happy Valley to stop suddenly amidst tall sal trees that grew in strange incongruity in the pine-scented forest. The rain continued to beat its musical dirge. In the depths of the forest sat a cottage of logwood, tin-roofed and stone-mounted. I inhaled the rain through the car window, letting my hair and face get wet, dreaming of long ago Sunday walks in Ashes Forest. By then Kong Bonili along with Kmie U Flin had waded bravely to the cottage. They were going to find out when they could meet Bah To, the nongpeit. Robert remained sitting at the wheel, drumming his fingers on the steering wheel, looking straight ahead.

I do not recollect how long it took, but I suddenly felt the car door slam and Kmie U Flin sat down heavily on the back seat. She was raving and ranting and Kong Bonili was consoling her. I looked at Robert. He was still looking straight but his drumming had ceased. He was silent and listening to what Kmie U Flin was saying. The nongpeit had refused to take up the case. There were only two other clients waiting but he had refused. She was furious.

We were now heading for Laban, Shillong's oldest locality spread on the slopes beyond the Garrison Ground. The Muslim baba's house was just beyond the little market. It had green walls and a wooden green gate that seemed to have weathered many a monsoon. The baba sat cross-legged in his prayer room that was decorated with gaudy pictures of mosques. He listened attentively, nodding his head understandingly now and again. The two plastic bags with the mud from the front and back of the gardener's cottage and the two used, still-damp towels recovered from the bathroom were placed by Kong Bonili in front of the baba. He first took one towel (Suresh's, I discovered later) and held it with both his hands, muttering under his breath as he blew into it, and then he said, 'This one is dead. He died a violent death for no fault of his.' Ignoring Kmie U Flin's tearful response he picked up Ravi's towel and repeated the procedure after which he said, 'This one is in deep trouble. He may also die. Yes, give me the mud. I will try and tell you who did it and how and why it happened.'

A young boy who was obviously an assistant of the baba brought two glasses of water. The glasses were then placed in front of the baba who muttered a mantra and put some mud from the first plastic bag (marked '1' by Titi to indicate that it was from the front of the house) into a glass of water. Then it all happened all at once, the quiet chants grew louder, the water in the glass turned red and I gasped and almost fainted. Kong Bonili screamed 'wawwaw' to express shock and agony and I went numb with fear. My teeth started to chatter uncontrollably. Then Kmie U Flin rose to her full height, her eyes glazed and fixed straight ahead.

The baba put a knife on her head and blew on it. 'The spirit of the dead boy is inside her. He will tell you what you want to know. You can also ask him any questions you wish to ask.'

I suddenly felt nauseous. My whole body felt like a block of ice and I stumbled out of the room, bumping into Robert as I did. Where had he been standing? Behind the door? I wouldn't know. I rushed to the car and leaned hard against it. Through half-closed eyes I saw Robert rushing inside the hut. I opened the car door and collapsed in the front seat.

As always, so typical of Shillong weather, the rain suddenly let up and the brightest of sunshine streamed through from a sky now turning deep blue and white. For a second, the world became beautiful again, a familiar world where murder occurred only in Agatha Christie novels. I revelled in it all for a long time, how long I wouldn't know, but somehow I managed to divert my mind completely from the bizarre situation. The car doors suddenly slammed shut. Robert slid into the driving seat. I looked back. Kmie U Flin was fast asleep, Kong Bonili had her eyes tightly shut. She was wide awake though. Her face was as white as a sheet.

Something was terribly wrong. Weighed down by secrets known and unknown, I started to cry.

33

Inside the tall white house with windows like hollow eyes, that rose above a cluster of hill cottages, red-roofed and innocent, the two men had just surfaced from a late night. Their eyes were puffy but alert and full of thoughts.

'Now let me get this straight, Ksan, the nongpeit cooperated with us but after that they went—where?'

'To some damn Mussalman in Laban and—God—I can't begin to tell you what happened there, according to… well, our reliable source.'

'For God's sake, just tell me… '

'The Mussalman called the spirit of Suresh Rai and it apparently told them everything.'

'No!'

'Yes, Strong, yes. Do these things really happen?'

'That's not the issue at the moment. Who all were there, who all heard is what is important.'

'Robert.'

'What about the old lady?'

'She was the medium so she wouldn't know.'

'What!'

'The medium never remembers. The friend or cousin, Kong whatever, heard everything but who'll believe her?'

'The point is even if the cops pick up bits and pieces as leads they are perfect leads. Where does Bonili stay? Find that out and also if there's a loyalist doctor in that vicinity.'

34

During the silent drive back home from the nongpeit and the Muslim baba I reeled under the most excruciating pangs of fear and guilt. How could I have fled during the most crucial moment at the baba's, why the hell had I gone if I was going to do such a stupid thing? How could I when I was, perhaps, the first and only witness to the crime? How could I when I'd already let Suresh and Ravi and Aibor and Aila down by not coming clean to the cops? How could I? How could I? But, I knew, life sometimes reaches a point when you can keep questioning yourself but there are really no answers.

When we reached home, Kong Bonili and Robert took Kmie U Flin to her room. I staggered into mine and passed out. I woke up to a still house with just the patter of a light drizzle. It was grey everywhere and I was famished. I went to the kitchen and prepared myself a huge brunch. Fried eggs sunny side up and sausages, a piece of roast chicken and some mashed potatoes from the fridge and a Cherrapunji banana, 'kait jaji', incomparable in its aroma and taste. I laid it out on the round dining table. The dull brownish-black shine of the teak wood and the rose petals fallen from the vase stared at me as I ate. I felt strangely soothed, mesmerized by the stillness and fragility of the petals, like autumn leaves carpeting the earth. I never allow the gardener to sweep away the leaves in my little Delhi back lawn, my private haven. The meal went down my gullet and settled comfortably inside my grateful stomach. I felt better.

I was sipping a steaming hot cup of coffee when Robert poked his head in through an open window.

'Oh Kong, I am so glad you are eating something. I don't think Kmie U Flin can make any lunch. I can get some Chinese food or jadoh from outside...'

'No thanks, I've just wolfed down a good brunch. I would now like to go out for a drive.'

'In this drizzle?'

'Yes. On the way you can have a jadoh feast.'

He broke into a grin, the brightest, happiest ever. If I'd known what lay ahead I'd have captured it on camera to illustrate the irony and travesty of life.

'By the way, Kong, Bah Aibor and Kong Aila are arriving day after tomorrow.'

'That's wonderful!'

I changed my clothes, slipping out of my caftan into a long skirt and polo neck sweater, and gathered my hair into a ponytail. Robert had brought the car out. I went to Kmie U Flin's room. Kong Bonili was sitting beside her slumbering friend and Titi was pressing her feet. I smiled at them and left.

'Robert, I want to go to the district jail.'

Silence.

'Robert, I want to go and see Ravi.'

'Kong, why don't you wait till Kong Aila arrives? We'll have to get permission.'

'I already have permission.'

Of course I didn't but I just wanted to take a chance and I wasn't going to spoil it by telling Robert the truth.

The jailer wasn't a Khasi, I could make that out. He was busy having an animated conversation on the phone and quite obviously very happy. His eye fell on me and he seemed to like what he saw. Cupping the mouthpiece, he asked me what I wanted. I said a little prayer and told him. He hollered for an assistant. I filled up a tattered register and before I knew it I was through.

The long, black, dark corridor of the jail seemed like an endless tunnel leading straight to hell. I felt as if I was walking though the insides of a serpent. I felt, quite simply, cold and terrible but I knew I could not back out. I had to make the trip.

The cell was dimly lit with an ancient cot on one side and the walls had blankness and despair inscribed everywhere. Ravi was hunched on the cot, smoking an unfiltered cigarette.

'Ravi.'

My voice sounded strange but steady and friendly. I felt as if I knew this person well, having seen him in that one instance on that misty evening filled with horror.

'Ravi.'

Still no response.

'Ravi, I know you didn't kill Suresh.' I spoke in Hindi.

The boy looked up. His eyes were filled with shock and fear. His mouth fell open. I felt faint. This was not the face I had seen. This was not Ravi.

'Who are you! You are not Ravi.'

I got no answer as his lips pursed tightly with a kind of ominous finality that made me shiver. I felt like an intruder in a world where scores had been settled, all payments made. I walked out. The jailor was still on the phone, laughing raucously.

The rain started again in torrents. The newspapers reported it as 'the highest rainfall in thirty years, probably caused by the depression in the Bay of Bengal.'

35

'The woman went to the jail.'

'I know.'

'She knows...'

'The Boss is thinking of what to do next.'

'Yeah. Good. When do we get a chance to think, as in think, anyway!'

'Thank God! The rain has let up a little. Be careful, Strong, don't slip. You've had a lot or what?'

There were not many strollers along the narrow path that rimmed the gorge just above the roaring waterfall. It was a working day and a misty morning, the ground slushy with leeches lurking in the tall grass. Inside the cave, naturally gated with two huge rocks and giant ferns, twenty or more men sat in council. Strong and Ksan entered amidst muffled greetings of Khublei, Khublei, Hi, Hello, nods, hands limply raised or just silent acknowledgements.

An hour later they emerged in twos and threes with a gap of ten or fifteen minutes in between and scampered up the hillside confidently. Most of them knew the terrain well. For some it was a childhood haunt where they had picnicked and hunted birds with catapults. Those who were not so confident of these wooded heights were cheerfully guided by fourteen-year-old Niro who had grown up on these slopes and still picked mushrooms and gathered wild herbs for his mother's kitchen. Just out of habit because, unlike earlier times, they now had plenty of meat and fish, vegetables and even fruit, all neatly stored in a brand-new fridge.

Niro was after all a workingman, a respected member of his family and the Organization. His work was to spy and wherever necessary, tell a few lies and spread some rumours for the benefit of the Boss. So what, his parents thought, at least someone in the family was working and earning well. Besides, wasn't the Organization working for the benefit of the people?

Like the last time Niro was told to stroll casually, kite in hand, and trick the police who were looking for a suspected militant.

He had overdone the details but the police were unsuspecting of the lad with a yellow kite and a curly mop atop a smiling face. As the jeep sidled up into the lane that led to the green-roofed cottage, someone threw a bomb. There was a loud, earsplitting explosion but the road remained empty. No crowds came rushing out. The police, caught in a situation they did not anticipate, left the scene, their mission incomplete. The militant was never caught.

Soon after, Niro's parents became proud owners of a sofa set, two beds (real wooden beds with springy Dunlop mattresses) and also a colour television. Life became almost strange, unbelievable to young Niro as he sat late into the nights transported to different worlds just with the press of a button. His mother invested in lengths of flowery curtains that billowed in cream, deep pink and mint green in the mountain breeze. She had, thankfully, progressed from grim resignation to hopeful cheer after the arrival of the fridge and even doubled up with laughter now and again. She started to hug and kiss Niro's younger siblings, filling their ears with unfamiliar murmurs.

Niro's father, Curtis, had been jobless for months, and before this turn in their fortunes, had started drinking to drown his sorrows. He had dreamt and prayed and hoped for a job in the soon-to-be constructed canning factory in the suburbs of the town. The plan was suddenly shelved, however, the funds ran out, they said. Same old story. Niro's father like everyone else knew the money must have gone towards realizing the desires and dreams of those who were privileged enough to be able to make their dreams become a reality. Brand-new cars, trips to exotic places with the entire family and servants in tow, gifts for the wife and children and mistresses—that was where the money always flowed, diverted like irrigation water.

So Niro's father walked out of his dream job to his mother's house. On the way he picked up his friend, Rodrick, who had suggested an encouraging alternative. Besides Rodrick was confident, articulate, a graduate, he would be able to put things across better than Niro's father. So his mother was told that a small provision store on the main road not far from his house was what they planned to setup. He wanted a loan. His mother said she did not have so much ready cash to which Niro's father suggested that she could dispose of some of the land at the foot of the garden. He would buy it from her. He had brought with him his wife's jewellery—everything she had—for security. His mother's impassive face suddenly twisted into a grimace and, seeing this, Niro's father put his hands together, fingers entwined on his slightly parted knees and let his mind go blank. Rodrick looked out of the window, waiting. Niro's grandmother popped some tobacco into her mouth and said, 'I don't know what you mean. What land? You have no share in this land. What has happened to this world, sons coming to their mothers demanding money? What is happening? Curtis, you ask your wife to ask her family. She has only one sister. Yes, I know she married you against her family's wishes but what can I do? It was your choice. What will your sisters say? And please, son, don't trouble your father. He is not well and, anyway, as you very well know this is not his property.'

Niro's father's heart sank and his hands felt clammy and cold. Rodrick and he finished their tea in silence and walked out onto a nothing pavement in a nothing world. They drank themselves into oblivion in a seedy bar and, till today, do not remember how they reached home.

Then, one day, Niro told them hesitantly that he had a job. The news was, as hesitantly, conveyed to Niro's mother who simply smiled and asked no questions. Niro suddenly looked grown up and developed a certain importance. He thanked God many times and actually attended church for three consecutive Sundays filled with deep gratitude, as did his parents.

Niro had spent the entire week in his usual haunts telling people about the robbery and murder in Bah Aibor's house. He stuck to the orders, embellishing the stories just enough to make the conversation interesting and yet leaving his listeners wondering and suitably disturbed.

36

'There are two days left for the bandh and a week away from August 15...'

'What is the slogan supposed to be?'

'You were dozing, I saw you.'

'I watched a movie till 3 a.m. Frankly I heard nothing.'

'Ok, ok. There's no slogan. They agreed on the Boss' strategy. Of course they think it's my strategy. They don't even know it is a strategy. They think it's the Ten Commandments straight from heaven. Same old thing...it's the reservation quota of seats, inner line permit, all that he told me at the meeting at the lake. Then of course, we stress on breaking away from Indian colonialism because of the callous neglect and...'

'Usual Delhi bashing but what are the guys here doing anyway! Clinging to their thrones that's all!'

'Got reports that in the Independence Day speech which the Prime Minister has prepared or rather—been prepared for the PM—there is no mention of the North East problems so good opportunity to come down hard...'

'What? Not even Nagaland and Manipur?'

'No'

'God! These Indian bastards don't give a damn. One day we'll just have to give in to our Big Brother from the East. It's between the Devil and the deep blue sea huh?'

'You can go for the Devil, I'll go for the deep blue sea. I can't dream of becoming a commie. Anyway, the plans for the next few days are chalked out and work has been delegated.'

'No police bashing again, I hope. How long can we use

them as punching bags? When are we going to come out clean, Strong? We are cowards. We Khasis have become cowards.'

'Ksan, stop chattering. I know you are rattled, so am I, but stop it, stop going off track. We have to go through with it and execute it meticulously…'

'What are you talking about? Go through with what?'

'God! You are the limit! I don't want to spell it out. It's too dangerous. Walls too have ears you know…'

'But you have to tell me…'

'Ok, let's go out. Let's go for a walk to the edge of the gorge. Let the wind carry the words away.'

Behind the green hills in the distance the sun was about to set. A Shillong sky after a heavy shower was always a treat. Silhouetted against the sky splashed with orange, purple, green and blue, stood Strong and Ksan, so still that it was almost as if they were part of the landscape.

'Strong, stop, stop. We are now attacking our own blood. What are you SAYING?'

'It's a war, man. All's fair in love and war. Say it once, Ksan, say it once to the wind. Once it is said half the deed is done, come on. We have to say it. SAY IT! The party is day after tomorrow. After that Miss Snoopy scoots back to Delhi.'

'No, I can't. I cannot sink to such a level.'

'Oh yeah? It isn't as if we have never killed. By the way, Kong Bonili died of a heart attack early this morning.'

'Huh?'

'She had some tea after dinner with some visitors from the locality. After that she went to sleep and never woke up.'

'Strong…'

'Yes?'

'We are SICK.'

37

The phone rang just when I'd finished dinner. Good dinner, smoked pork cooked with onions, garlic, tomatoes and bamboo shoot, dried fish chutney sprinkled with jamyrdoh and red hill rice.

'Kong, thank you. This meal is out of this world,' I told Aila's cousin, who had come to help with the cooking.

'Tomorrow I'll cook fish for you, hilsa in mustard oil, steamed with onion, nei lieh and green chillies and pepper. It is a Bengali dish but I believe you like it very much,' she answered cheerfully.

I knew they were all trying their best to keep me happy and Kmie U Flin had managed to give instructions in spite of the trauma.

The phone rang. I raced for it thinking it was Aila. It wasn't.

'May I speak to Raseel Babbar?'

'Speaking.'

It was one of Aibor's friends, a minister. He said he had just come to know about my visit and he was sorry about all the trouble and the inconvenience caused by the robbery. He would like to invite me to his residence for dinner the following day. It was his wife's birthday but no presents please! Transport would be arranged.

'Anything else I can do for you, Raseel?'

'Well, yes, Bah, I went to the district jail yesterday to visit Ravi, the suspect. I am quite sure that the young man incarcerated is not Ravi.'

'Pardon? I don't quite get you.'

I knew that that was not true but he was buying time for the right response. So I repeated what I had said out of deference for his position and out of anxiety for my own.

'Really? This is certainly very serious. I'll look into it. I'll ring up the SP at once. Anything else? You are really quite an amazing girl.'

'I don't think it's a simple case of robbery at all. In fact I am quite sure of that too.'

'Raseel, I am a friend of Aibor's and you are his guest. You've come for a holiday—do you want to get involved in all this mess? You don't have to feel guilty, I'll sort it out.'

I kept silent. I was shocked.

'I can understand how you feel. We'll talk about it tomorrow. In the meantime I'll contact the SP straightaway.'

I told Kmie U Flin about the invitation. It brought her out of her shock and grief over Kong Bonili's sudden demise. Her swollen red eyes lit up a little at the thought of my being invited by the minister. I hugged her tight. I didn't know what else to do. I had been doing that all day ever since I got the news. I was somewhat thankful for the natural death. Her hearing everything the 'spirit' had to say had endangered her and I had been scared and miserable.

'Kong, you must wear a dress, a long dress. You will look beautiful, your hair you leave open but pin it back like Sonia Gandhi.'

'Good lord! A long dress...'

'Yes, all right, not so long, a mini.'

'What? I thought you said long...'

'She means midi, Kong.'

It was Robert.

Robert had just entered the room. Kmie U Flin looked down at her toes shyly. I hugged her again. In that one instance I felt the burden of her sadness.

'Ok, a midi.'

'Yes, good, Kong—a dress.'

'Accha, I get you. Desi saris and salwars are not approved here. Aila had told me but I forgot. But I'm going to a private party, an exclusive gathering.'

'Kong, Meisan is right. They are everywhere and watching, please wear something safe—tribal or western is best.'

'I know very little about dressing. I asked Kong Aila one day about the dress she was wearing...I told her that if she wore a Punjabi dress she would look like Juhi Shawla...yes, she would.'

Robert looked pensive and suddenly said, as if he was speaking to himself,

'We are all Indians but the rest of India knows nothing about us, they call us Assamese.'

'Robert, the north Indians call everyone from the south Madrasis and when you go south, the south Indians call everyone from the north Punjabis.'

'Where does Kanodia come from, Kong Raseel?

'Kanodia is a Marwari. He comes from Rajasthan in north-west India.'

Kanodia owned the huge provision store from which the household got its monthly supplies. He, like the rest of his community, owned all the large shops in Shillong along with the Sindhis, although the Sindhis concentrated on readymade garments. Their shops stood out because of their excellent window-dressing. In 1863, Shillong become the capital of the Khasi and Jaintia hills. In 1864, Police Bazaar was founded with the setting up of a departmental store, Ghulam Haider and Sons. A hundred years later, when I was a young school girl, it housed Modern Book Depot in its place. My parents and I frequented Abdul Ghaffoor and Sons, which was set up in 1872 when Shillong become the capital of Assam. I used to love going there and revelling in the different aromas of soaps and powders, stationery, toys, handkerchiefs, biscuits, toffees, an endless array of goodies, everything except booze and cigarettes. Below Abdul Ghaffoor was Jamatullah and his tailoring shops. My first grown up, no- frills dress was beautifully stitched by him. After that, they say, came the big Marwari traders and merchants, the Singhanias and the Goenkas. Some of their children were in school with us. The Marwaris were closely followed by the Bengalis like the Ghosal Brothers who set up book stalls and photo studios. In 1905, when Nawab Bahadur Kasimuddin started the first taxi service between Shillong and Gauhati (now Guwahati) motor workshops sprang up. Khan Motors was walking distance from our beautiful bungalow in the nearby cantonment area so we patronized the workshop quite frequently. After that, we'd take the longish walk to Morello's and have a cup of tea with slices of sponge cake and the most delicious chicken sandwiches.

Kmie U Flin and Robert listened enraptured as I recounted it all; most locals didn't know all this but I did because I loved reading and travelling and Shillong. By then I had decided what to wear. A calf-length skirt, slim-fit top with long sleeves, my natural colour pashmina and cherry-coloured Lotus Bawa shoes. How 'Delhi girl', I felt, and smiled inwardly.

The phone rang. It was Aila!

'Ras, Ras how are you? We heard about the ghastly incident.'

'Where are you, you crazy girl?'

'We're in Cal. From China we went all over, that's why we missed the messages. No, no one messaged the details—they thought it would be too much. Aibor and I felt so terrible...'

'Don't worry, Aila. I've been through enough to be prepared for this. Just tell me—when are you arriving? I'm longing to see you.'

'Ras, day after, positively. Aibor has some important work in Cal...but he has talked to everyone concerned... and my brothers are there to handle it so don't worry. I have to be here, you know the usual boring entertainment one has to go through. Life for us business types is never easy. I am longing to get back, Ras, and give you a proper holiday.'

'I'm rather enjoying my improper one!'

'Oh, Ras, you are so full of beans. How's Kmie U Flin? She adored those boys. Oh God! That reminds me. I must get a proper prayer done in that cottage to cleanse it of the tyrut.'

'The what?'

'Tyrut…it's a kind of curse resulting from any violent death. It attacks generation after generation unless it is cleansed. We are Christians but I'd still like to get it done. Ras, you are so strong. I'd have run off the day after that ghastly…'

'I can't Aila, I'm too deeply involved.'

'Involved?'

'Yes, I…well, I sort of saw almost the whole crime. The boy they've locked up is not your garden help, Ravi. Aila, there is some terrible mistake somewhere. This is something very, very wrong. I saw the murderers, Aila. I can even identify one…Aila?'

There was no response.

'Aila?'

'Yes, Ras.' A whisper. 'I am sorry. Ras, please just take care till we come. I am really sorry.'

'Aila, don't be sorry, you crazy girl. You had warned me that things here are bad…just finish your work then come, ok? Bye.'

'Bye. Ras, listen, think about it. If you want to leave right away you can come to Cal. We can meet here…'

'No, Aila, let's meet here as planned.'

'Ok, then bye, let me know if…'

'Ok, ok, Aila. Bye.'

I watched television for a while then tried to read, making the sofa, sheathed in English upholstery, my bed. I don't know when I fell asleep with *The Idea of India* on my chest, resting precariously, half read.

I was shaken out of my slumber by the sound of shattering glass in my room which was next door. As I opened the door the night wind rushed in through the broken window panes, tearing angrily at the mosquito net around my bed that had been lowered for the night. I switched on the light. On the bedside rug was a huge stone. It had, obviously, failed its mission.

I leaned against the door, took three deep breaths then switched off the lights and went back to the reading-cum-TV room. I gulped a Valium with a glass of water and fell into a deep sleep, wrapped up in a huge Naga shawl. Before I did, however, I recorded a small detail that snuggled into my mind throughout my conversation with Aila: someone was listening on the extension.

38

The following morning, I firmly told the entire staff that, in spite of the previous night's incidents, we were not going to do a thing until Aila and Aibor returned. Then I drove out and spent the whole morning and afternoon in the beauty parlour in Laitumkhrah. The owner of the upmarket salon treated me to chicken patties and espresso coffee from the new bakery in town and supplied me with Davidoff cigarettes from her Christian Dior bag. I returned from a most satisfying session and sank into a much-needed siesta. By seven I had showered and felt on top of the world. Kmie U Flin brought me a concoction of brandy, hot water, honey and lemon to protect me against the chills that always set in when one bathed in the evening in the hills.

I had moved up to the first floor, to a room with a different view—no pear orchard, no gardener's cottage but a quiet benign slope landscaped Japanese style with a circular pond at the bottom surrounded with irises of purple and moonlight white.

I dressed with care and totally in keeping with the advice of the wise old one of the house.

The SP looked appreciatively at me as he took my statement. I was startled by his presence in the hallway as I sailed down the staircase. I glared at Robert for going against my orders but he had his duties and I understood. It was obvious, after the inspection of the grounds outside, that the intruder could not have traversed miles for he was barefoot and he also knew where to aim, at the window closest to my bed. The SP posted two guards for my benefit and left.

I took a deep breath and tried to forget last night's events.

On the way to Princeton Lyngwa's house I passed the erstwhile Polo Grounds, now a huge stadium for soccer and hockey. An eyesore if one compared it to what it had once been, a beautifully kept patch of emerald green encircled by wooden stiles and the turf for the races. Races outlived polo, the game that originated in neighbouring Manipur. During my girlhood days I used to love coming to the races because my mother would be at her sunniest best, laughing and betting with her Khasi friends. My father did not know of this delicious, surreptitious indulgence of hers. As the car dipped and then climbed up to the minister's house, I could almost hear that tinkling laughter of hers and my eyes smarted. I was grateful that the August night wrapped me in its cover. The darkness completely blanketed the Umkhrah stream, now no longer a sparkling hill stream full of cheer but a sluggish sewer choked with the city's filth. Does anyone even consider Nature's feelings when they indulge in such carelessness? Don't they know that the wrath of Nature surpassed all great emotions? I mourned for the many things lost forever.

The enormous wooden bungalow nestled amidst a brotherhood of tall pines. The red pine verandah shone like only a Khasi house can shine and the aroma of recent polish wafted to the car as we drove into the porch. In true Delhi style, I began to arrange my thoughts and feelings, juggled up appropriate but not bright conversation starters and fixed my face to a near-perfect expression of delight and joie de vivre. Deep inside of course, my heart churned with inexplicable emotions. I told Robert to go home and relax. I decided to take up the minister's offer and get dropped home. I wanted to be as free and as far away as possible from last week's events.

As soon as the car halted a tall, striking young man walked up to the car to welcome me. I couldn't help but notice the well-cut suit and inhale the expensive cologne he wore as his handsome face split into a grin.

'Good evening, ma'am.'

'Khublei.'

'Oh yes, khublei, khublei.'

Khublei (kyrkhu u Blei) meant God bless you. It was the traditional form of greeting when Khasis met one another and while parting and also when they thank. It was the first Khasi word we learnt when we came to Shillong. We learnt it from our first maid, Rimon.

The young man introduced himself as the minister's eldest son. He smiled a great deal and I could not help noticing his even teeth and healthy pink lips and his hair that shone like copper. It was obvious that some time somewhere along the line an Englishman had stormed into the family genes. Great looks, great education—Bangalore, New Delhi, East Coast, USA, where he was graduating in economics the following year. One sister was doing hotel management in Sydney and another studying in an exclusive boarding school in Mussoorie. I was glad I had quizzed Robert about my host and his family. It made everything easier for me.

We stepped into the lawn where people sat in circles around elegant tables covered in white tablecloths. Napkins, crockery, flowers, tables, chairs were all whistle-clean white. Some guests stood around the bar, chatting, a drink in hand. The minister walked up to me followed by his arrestingly beautiful wife, a shorter version of Catherine Zeta-Jones. He was not so bad either with his antiquated charm which went exceedingly well with his pipe and Louis Armstrong voice. Everything seemed perfect but I felt something was not quite right.

'So many guests. There is even one in a turban,' I heard myself say, my voice faltering and then sitting, unmoving in my throat.

'Yes,' the minister's wife responded, fingering her off-white pearls that matched her dhara. 'That's Bah Ibanmanik. He is one of our ministers, also a chieftain, a syiem.'

In the Khasi hills there are big states, 'himas', and smaller ones, 'elakas'. A hima is ruled by the syiem who is elected from the royal clan by the myntris (the ministers) who are representatives of the important clans of the hima. To this day all these rulers have special administrative and judicial powers. The British did not conquer the Khasi Hills but signed treaties with the syiems.

'Come Raseel, let's go and meet him.'

The waiter came by with a tray of drinks. I picked up

another gin and lime and gulped it. The minister's sister-in-law, Joyce, walked up to me and put her hand around my waist like an old friend.

'Let's not rush to meet Iban as if we are fans,' she laughed. 'He is damn handsome but will he hand us some?' I doubled up with laughter at this small joke, so grateful for the respite.

Ibanmanik Singh definitely had his fans. Of medium height and athletic-looking, his bespectacled handsome face sported a moustache and an attractive mien of great confidence.

'He's a minister, look at his strut. He walked so regally earlier but now he struts.'

'Joyce, I believe the youth here, the young men especially, are very dissatisfied with the system. Sad isn't it and what...'

'Yes, there's lot of trouble but what's so sad? These boys are just causing all this mayhem for lack of better things to do.'

'I don't think so. I don't think so at all. The young men and women involved couldn't be enjoying it at all.'

'Oh yes, they are and why not? Monsters! They are having a whale of a time, easy money, drug- or drink-induced happiness, plenty of sex, no real responsibilities. Anyway, my husband and I are Khasis but we live far from this hellhole in Cal. We come twice a year to see everyone and see to our properties, we enjoy ourselves and zip off...'

I was stunned. I popped a chicken wonton into my mouth from a passing tray.

'They used to make better wontons, those Chinese,

now they've all left.' Joyce licked her finger delicately as her diamonds glittered unabashedly.

'Why have they left?'

I wasn't really interested but I couldn't possibly be silent as my eyes roamed all over the place, trying to see why I was feeling so uneasy.

'Extortion and all that. For the cause, hah! Delinquents! Thank God my kids are in Pune in decent schools in decent company…'

'Because you can afford it, Joyce. Those so-called delinquents can't.'

It was just then that there was a loud commotion and two gunshots. In a turbulence of flapping wings some resting birds rose above the trees and fled. Joyce caught my hand and started praying. Scores of policemen appeared from nowhere and converged towards the gate.

It couldn't have taken long because the taste of the wonton still lingered in my mouth.

The minister's son came striding towards me and holding me by the shoulders, said quietly, 'Come, don't worry. It was an intruder. Yes, a Khasi. Must have been drunk but one can't risk it.'

He led me to a room where a friend's son was playing Beethoven's 'Fur Elise', as if nothing had happened. A waiter brought a tray of drinks. I took another gin and tonic and took huge gulps.

Next morning the headlines in the local newspaper shrieked, 'SHOOTING IN MINISTER'S HOUSE'. The guards, a Khasi and Garo, had been shot. No one was caught. The law and order situation in the state has plummeted to dismal depths, said the report.

39

It was noon by the time I woke up and Aila was home. My spirits soared like a kite as I tumbled out of bed and quickly got ready. She looked wonderful after her holiday, a luxury cruise from Hong Kong to Zhanjiang and then on to Halong Bay. In Haikou, capital of China's Hainan Island, the 'Hawaii of the Orient', she had made a wonderful discovery: that she was not as in love with her husband as she thought, she confided in me. A few months before the cruise, she got wind of her husband's infidelity. She had called me up then, and wept copiously, blaming it on her barrenness. In the same breath she cited umpteen examples of men who had a football team at home but yet who strayed. I had sold the idea of Star Cruises to her and advised her to go find herself.

'I am feeling great, Ras.'

She stretched her lithe body languidly as her Tods slipped off her small perfect feet.

'Aila, you are looking absolutely wonderful. I am so happy.'

'Ok, now ask me why I am so happy or rather, guess…'

'What's there to guess? Obviously Aibor got down on his knees and confessed most ardently that it's you and you alone.'

'Wrong. Guess again.'

'He said there was no such thing as an affair, that it was all a terrible mistake.'

'Wrong again.'

'Ok, he said he fantasized about you right through making love to whoever it was.'

'Oh! Wrong, Ras, wrong.'

'I give up.'

'Aibor confessed to the whole thing, apologized profusely and promised it'll never ever happen again. He's typical, darling, typical.'

'Uhhuh.'

'I looked at him and I saw everything clear as day. So I pointed it out to him that he was not sorry but simply waiting for another opportunity once I'm thrown completely off scent. *This* piece of drama, I said, was in honour of *that*.'

'Good lord!'

'He said I was crazy. I told him I was honest. I told him, there where we were sitting in this unbelievably beautiful beach in Haikou, so beautiful and pristine—how could we soil it all with lies—on top of that lies to ourselves and to each other.'

'Aila, you are amazing…'

I didn't know what else to say. My head was full of other thoughts.

Aila's feet now rested on the mula, the ubiquitous cane stool, as her eyes roamed all over her weedy, monsoon garden, sprayed with colour by a rebellious gulmohur and a quiet jacaranda. Aila was exceptionally attractive and different. She, the daughter of an Irish tea planter's son and a high-born Khasi lady, had inherited her father's sparkling green eyes and her mother's high cheek bones and long, straight hair. She never let things get her down for long. At school, she had been good at sports and dramatics and also won all the elocution and debate trophies. Those were the halcyon days when there was no unwritten blanket rule that all children should shine in academics or else. If you did—wonderful, if you did not, the teacher tried to find something else special within the child. Aila, in spite of her continual fifty percents, was a star and being of mixed blood and Catholic also helped tremendously in a convent. She knew it and had a ball all through school without ever being brash, that inimitable grace, so much like Aunty Rosamon.

'Ras, now you tell me everything that has happened. Or should we wait for Aibor? He rushed off straight for his office. Just grabbed some fruit and his sweater and off he went. He looked so tired…Yeah, there's so much violence here, Ras. If you go to a public place you can feel it in the air. A cousin of mine—you know her, Adriana—she and her entire family have moved out of their ancestral home in Mawkhar.'

'That beautiful home? What happened?'

'Well, one night they heard some commotion outside in the street so they switched off the lights and peeped—the usual procedure here. There was a group of boys around a dkhar boy who had fallen and they were stoning him. He was covered in blood but they wouldn't stop. She called the cops but it was too late. They came only to collect a mass of flesh—someone's child, brother, husband, friend, Ras. They said they kept hearing that awful sound, pchaak pchaak, of someone being hacked and blood spurting out, for months on end. Can you imagine? Ras, I am so ashamed of my community.'

'I can, Aila, I can but we'll wait for Aibor then I'll tell you. I can't do it twice.'

'Oh!' she chirped and her forehead smoothened.

'But you are not involved in all this, are you, Aila? You and Aibor?'

Aila made no reply. I knew she wasn't keen to know. I didn't press. We lapsed into silence, staring at the sky and beyond. Yet I was scared. Even when my parents were murdered and I returned home to a strange flat filled with incense and relatives, I did not feel this cold, clammy terror. Maybe because I arrived three days later and my uncles did not wait for me to be part of the last rites because of the heat. I cried for many weeks, any time, any place, and shivered with the thought of the double murder but I did not feel like I felt now. Maybe because then I knew who the criminal was and who were the victims. This time I didn't.

I knew I couldn't go through another trauma again. I must clear my doubts, there were just too many. I looked at Aila, ready to ask her to come out clean. She was looking at me and she was crying. I went up to her and whispered 'Aila, tell me.'

'Ras, we are in deep shit, we are involved. Aibor was so keen to get a contract, not so much for the money but the idea of making this Amusement Park for the children, a contribution to the state by someone from here. That was our focus. We travelled all over India and the US, UK, Singapore to pick up ideas. The Minister promised him but at a price…'

'So you all actually let what happened, happen? You knew they were going to…Ravi…Suresh…Aila, how could you?'

'Aibor said they promised that they would not… that they would only rough them up, rob and at the most kidnap and then let them go but Suresh started to threaten. Oh God! It is all so terrible. I don't know, I don't really know, I don't remember but it was something like that, Ras. How did we get into this mess, Ras—how, how? A murder in my house, oh my God! I can't believe it, Ras. Is it all about wanting more and more? No, no it was not, Ras. It was not! We wanted to contribute something good…but, yes, Aibor gave in to that man's evil designs and I couldn't stop him. Robert and him… they convinced me. My God! Am so worried Ras…Am so…I don't know what, Ras…'

'And Ravi?'

'He escaped but they arrested another Bihari boy apparently. Some deal was made with his family—big money and all that. Please Ras don't ask anymore. Please. I can't…'

I held her for a long time. I don't remember how long.

40

'The stone did not scare the Delhi woman. Kong Aila and Bah have returned.'

'I know. I wonder what the Boss will do next. The CM has resigned so he gets full marks there but I believe Aibor didn't get the contract to build the Amusement Park. Aibor, I believe, is wild. He is fuming.'

'What a scum, the Boss is…How could he do this? Why didn't he see to it that Bah Aibor, a Khasi, got the contract? He's been making full use of him, even staging this whole crime in Bah's house.'

'I had heard that the Marwari had given thirty, forty crores or something like that but…'

'I heard that Bah Aibor has threatened to spill the beans.'

'No! That's so bloody dangerous…for Aibor. God! I'm not feeling good about this, Ksan.'

'Nor am I.'

41

Lunch was served in the verandah on a three-tiered rosewood trolley. Aila had calmed down and, although I was reeling under shock, I decided to divert her thoughts and my own. I desperately needed to. I tossed and turned quite a few ideas in my mind before I settled on a topic. I'd begin gently, I thought, at the beginning.

'Aila, your maternal grandpa fought for a separate hill state, didn't he?'

'Oh yes, he didn't stand for elections and all that but he was very much a stalwart in the movement. I'll never forget the chant "We want hill state, no hill state no rest." We got this separate state in my last year of school—a year after you left. You know it was quite traumatic for me, frankly, because my parents stopped me from going over to Shikha Mukherjee's. Yes, yes, imagine! Just because she was a Bengali—I remember that last Durga Puja I watched the festivals in her house sitting in my attic and crying. For years I was part of it all, even Mei and Pa used to go over for the feast. Part of me was severed just like that. The Mukherjees sold the house and left and Shikha eventually finished her studies from Darjeeling. She couldn't bear Cal, having grown up in the hills all her life. Some rich people from Jaintia Hills have bought the house now. It looks different, brightly painted and flooded with potted plants. The smells and the sounds are different. We still share the same hedge. I miss my old life, my old friends, Ras. Remember Hillaire Belloc?'

And we recited together in the now lambent light—*From quiet homes/ and first beginnings/ Out to the undiscovered ends/ there's nothing worth/ the wear of winning/ but laughter and/ the love of friends.*

It was then that we saw a fleet of cars coming down the driveway. Slowly, very slowly they purred to a stop for what seemed like an eternity, while Aila and I froze and wondered. Nobody stepped out of the cars. Two white Ambassadors, Aibor's Mercedes, a Zen and a Willys jeep stopped in a straight line on the slope, still, very still. Then, two ladies stepped out. I recognized one as Aila's mother's sister, Aunty Irene. Aila's father emerged next and walked down with his wife, Aila's stepmother, her face so pale, geisha white. They stared at us and we stared back then suddenly Aila screamed, a scream I'll never forget, and flew into her aunt's arms. She knew, even before they told her, that she had lost the one person who she tried so hard to stop loving but failed.

Aibor was dead. He was waylaid and shot thrice in the head while returning home from his office. Strangely, the incident took place on the lovely road that climbs up from Polo Ground to the pine-scented locality on top. It was the longest road to the house. Aibor used a different route home, we would never know why. They shot Robert too. Robert was also dead. Simultaneously, 'Ravi Rai' conveniently managed to procure some poison and was found dead in his miserable cell. Suresh's body was never found. The cops, however, identified the long navy blue airbag found at the bottom of the cliff below the house because of an inland letter addressed to Suresh, his father's last letter to a beloved son and a major contributor to the family's meagre income.

The sudden, unexpected turn of events, the enormity of the tragedy completely shattered me. I knew for certain that this time I would not be able to cope.

That night, I rang up Renu Masi and Vinny. The following day Vinny and her fiance, Vijay, arrived. They stayed for the three-day mourning period. They did all they could to help Aila get over the loss of a husband and me the loss of a world I had clung onto for so long and now, no longer knew. They knew it was a world I had earlier needed to return to again and again to maintain my sanity. They knew my loss was almost as great as Aila's.

Aibor was dead. I couldn't even say 'hello' after so many years of not meeting. From the airport he went straight to 'work' except for those few minutes at home when he picked up his sweater. Aila came home to be with me, to participate in what now seemed a perfect epilogue, her eyes filled with the secret knowledge that she could not share. I had sensed that and felt strange and sad for it was so unlike Aila. The falseness hung on her like an ill-fitting gown. I watched her from a distance amidst flowers and condolences, breaking down now and again, filling the house with cries of despair which broke my heart.

Aunty Irene, Uncle Ken, her husband, and almost a dozen relatives had moved in for the mourning period. Aibor's body lay in a tent outside while the locality boys and male relatives kept vigil all night. Since he died an unnatural death his body was not brought inside the house. I didn't get a chance to see Robert for he was taken straight to his mother's place. I didn't want to dwell on the deaths. I had said goodbye the night before, to everyone, in my mind. To Robert too, I had said goodbye the night before. I wrote down Hillaire Belloc's poem and put the paper on Aibor's cold chest. I sent one to Robert too through a relative. *From quiet homes/ and first beginnings/ out to the undiscovered ends/ there's nothing worth/ the wear of winning/ but laughter and/ the love of friends.*

I loved them both in different ways for, like me they were people in pain, pain that would now continue for many more lifetimes. And they were both my childhood friends and, to me, wonderful men caught in circumstances beyond their control as they both played their karmic games. Maybe they were wrong. Maybe they were right. I wouldn't know. In the church where the service was held I prayed that they would, one day, wake up into a world, a rose garden, their dreams fulfilled.

At that point in time I didn't realize I was praying for so many others too.

I wept until I felt nothing but complete and irreversible emptiness inside, like a tiny egg shell, fragile, inconsequential.

On the fourth day, I left along with Vijay and Vinny. I said my goodbyes and hugged Kmie U Flin for a long time, knowing that I would never see her again.

42

Almost half way to Guwahati is the tiny village of Nongpoh. Once you leave the hills of Shillong and its surrounding areas and dip into smaller valleys and lower hills you stumble upon this town with its busy eating places and shops crammed on either side, jostling for space. I was startled to see the hermaphrodite in the first stall. Kong It (as we had always called him) had been there since my school days and didn't seem to have aged much. We were all famished and Vinny and Vijay strode without hesitation to the nearest tea shop—a wooden shack painted black with mobile oil and a black tin roof but fronted with the most gorgeous array of flower pots bursting with colour. The steps were of rough stone, casually put together, they shook wearily as we stepped on them into the dhaba filled with smoke and morning sunbeams. I strolled in casually with them and sat on a bench long enough for three, the table wide enough for six but pushed against a window with a view of the rolling hills outside.

Then I saw him at the next table. The sun slanted on his leucoderma face, lighting up his eyes that looked silently outwards. He was strumming his guitar and singing a Bob Dylan song.

Everyone wants to know why he couldn't adjust
Adjust to what—a dream that bust?
He was a clean-cut kid

But they made a killer out of him
That's what they did.
They said what's up is down, they said what isn't is,
They put ideas in his head, he thought were his.
He was a clean cut kid
But they made a killer out of him
That's what they did.

'What a morbid song to sing early in the morning,' Vinny grimaced, eating a plate of noodles mixed with raw tomatoes, chillies and onions cut very small, Shillong style.

How would she know that for the singer there was no morning, no night, only bewildering hours inhabited by the spirits of slaughtered dreams? I remembered Robert and I stretched out my hand to touch him but he wasn't there.

They gave him dope to smoke, drinks and pills
A jeep to drive, blood to spill.
He was a clean-cut kid
But they made a killer out of him
That's what they did.

They said, congratulations, you got what it takes
They sent him back to the rat race
Without any brakes.
He was a clean-cut kid
But they made a killer out of him
That's what they did.

I stepped out into the ordinariness of a Wednesday morning. He continued strumming his guitar, he continued to sing.

Well everybody's asking why he couldn't adjust

Adjust to what—a dream that bust?
All he ever wanted was someone to trust.
He never did know what it was all about.
He was a clean-cut kid
But they made a killer out of him

If I had turned around I would have met his eyes but I didn't. But everything became clear to me like the opening of the Third Eye.

Epilogue

They say that people, places, communities and countries too, have their karmas to go through .

Last year, four years after the tragedy, Aila suddenly arrived in Delhi without notice and said she wanted to go to a place she had never been before.

In Jodhpur, leaning against the ramparts of the magnificent fort she told me that things were much better now in Shillong. She told me without my asking. She knew as she always did what was most foremost in my mind.

Everything and everyone?

Ho oid, she whispered. Yes.

And in that one word I found great comfort.

THE FLIGHT

The Flight

Mawii sat under the shade of the lemon tree, deep in thought, so deep it was almost a half sleep. Never before in her eighteen years did she ever have to face a dilemma such as this. Such a huge decision had to be made all on her own because nobody was willing to give her the support she needed. Not that she flaunted her affair, obviously not. In a small town like Aizawl, however, and if you are attached to a well-known household, tongues wag, eyes see and ears hear more than they should. So everyone would look at her with crooked smiles, unspoken words and eyes squinting with unkind thoughts. Even Hmingthani, who was also a help in the household of the elegant Kapi Lalpeki Khiangte, had very categorically told her that a decision such as this had to be made alone. To run away with someone was risky enough but to elope with Zakir Sheikh was pure suicide. 'Nobody is going to say "yes" for sure and they know saying "no" is a waste of breath with you young people. Especially you, you don't even like going to church. You are the pits. Decide for yourself, you silly girl. I cannot believe anyone would fall in love with a vai, and that, too, with that particular lot of vais. You are so mawl, so, so naive,' she hissed, storming away puffing her cigarette.

Mawii did not cry, she just stared at the elder help. Deep inside she knew Hmingthani had known love and she understood. Yet, again, how could she encourage

Mawii in this particular case? A married man, okay, a cousin too close to marry, okay, a drunkard, okay, a guy without a job, okay, an alleged bisexual, okay, but a vai—a plainsman, a non-tribal, and a Muslim vai at that—no way. She would be ostracized and maybe even beaten up for abetting such a crime. Mawaii understood but she was sad.

Hmingthani was almost fifteen years older than Mawii and to Mawii she was very wise and confident. She had studied up to Class Seven and she could read and write Mizo and scrawl some English words in her shopping list. She was far more educated than Mawii's aunt, Nu Sangi, who brought her up and lived in a small village near Lungleh. She was Mawii's only close living relative. Two years with an Assamese family in a tea estate in Silchar had furthered enhanced Hmingthani's innate sophistication and ways. She knew how to serve tea in a tray, make payash and fish tenga, wear kaajal and do namaskar. Hmingthani was Mawii's undisputed heroine. Mawii wished she had been more supportive but she knew it would go against the elder's portrayal of herself as a decent and sensible person. Her stern Christian upbringing must be pricking her conscience at just the thought of having to share such a terrible secret.

The afternoon was giving way to a sultry evening for it was a warm April in Aizawl. A quiet breeze wafted by and Mawii inhaled the tangy aroma of ripening lemons, yellowing in the sun. She kept inhaling till she emerged out of her reverie and her head felt light and clear. It was almost five o'clock and soon she would resume her duties and serve tea to the grand old lady, her widowed daughter Rinpuii, who lived with her and Kapi's still handsome and dapper seventy-five year-old cousin, Kapu Zoram, who they said was her secret lover. Mawii did not think so. She had seen them both watching TV holding hands, not holding actually but one hand resting on the other. They looked so comfortable and so much love flowed between them like two good friends who understood each other utterly and completely. Sex caused complications and Mawii was sure that they were not lovers. Mawii was quite startled by her thoughts but they came to her so easily, like water from a spring so she felt she was right and, for some reason, she was happy with the thought.

Hmingthani, who would have said 'sex binds', had baked a cake and Mawii was to fry some papad just before tea was served. Kapi loved papads, a habit she had developed in Tamil Nadu where her late husband, a Central Service officer, was posted long ago. 'They eat it with their meal or after a meal but I like it at tea time,' she would explain to her visitors who were curious to taste the new delicacy, all curly and crispy. Kapi's dinners were, of course, always the talk of the town, gourmet dishes on a meticulously set table. The guests would be treated to a hearty Mizo meal of steaming boiled rice, arsabusiar, ratwai, samtok, karela leaves and tender garlic, saptheinah, passion fruit leaves, bamboo shoot dal, aidoo with potato and either a pork or beef stew. Sometimes a Continental or Chinese meal would be on the menu and it would be so perfect that it could comfortably compete with the best restaurants in Shillong.

As Mawii stretched and tidied her clothes before resuming duty she thought, how could Nu Lmingthani be so cruel, whatever it was, how could she? A suicidal match, she had said. Why compare it to such a tragic thought? Just because he was not Mizo? Zakir hailed from Assam which was so close by, he even spoke Mizo and he was known to be the best carpenter Aizawl had ever seen. She heard Kapi Lalpeki tell all her visitors about Zakir's skills. That was how she met him: when Kapi was constructing an extension to her house because she needed an extra room when Rinpuii moved in. Zakir did all the woodwork along with two Bihari assistants.

Mawii fell in love the minute she set eyes on him as she served midday tea and sweet rusks to all the workers. He didn't see her immediately. In fact, for the first two days when she served tea, he had taken his mug and rusk without looking up. She watched him as he sipped his tea reflectively, his long eyelashes resting lightly on his lower eyelids like soft, wild ferns. Mawii had fallen in love with his eyes, the colour of his skin like burnished gold and his quiet, untutored indifference. 'Mawii, I saw everything. The way you looked at that vai. You are doomed,' Hmingthani had said, lighting her after-lunch Capstan, shaking her head, pursing her lips.

On the third day Mawii could contain herself no longer so while serving his tea she said to him, 'Here, take two rusks. You look hungry.' Zakir had slowly lifted his eyes, as if he was timing himself and then their eyes met. His light amber eyes took in her coal black stare, bold yet innocent, amused but nervous. He found the confusion of emotions intoxicating. Hmingthani saw it all and berated Mawii throughout the day and told her that all she was doing was inviting trouble and great unhappiness. She was genuinely concerned.

'But we had not even spoken a word. Why are you so agitated?'

'I saw the way you both looked at each other yesterday and today. Oof! Go back to the village. I am going to report you to your aunt.'

'Oh no, Nu! How can you? I will explain to her myself…'

'About impending disaster in her family?' Hmingthani began, then she stopped, remembering that her aunt had suffered greater disaster at the hands of the soldiers during the long years of rebellion. 'Maybe it is the luck of this family,' she ruminated, taking a long drag from her cigarette and exhaling slowly, trying to ward off unpleasant thoughts of village traumas during her own childhood, years ago.

Mawii didn't hear a word for she was already in her own world. After two long weeks filled with longing, Zakir Sheikh touched her hand while she handed him the cup of tea. That was it. After lunch she snuggled up to Hmingthani like a small child and holding her tenderly by the elbow told her, 'I am in love. Very much in love, Nu Mathani.' Hmingthani jerked her hand away and without saying a word walked away briskly out of the compound onto the main road, disappearing into the crowd. She knew Hmingthani had to do it but she felt hurt, wounded. She sat on her haunches and wept under the lemon tree, bathed in sunlight.

Thoughts crowded her mind, bumping into each other ceaselessly as she wept, sad, confused and fearful, tears coursing down her cheeks. Zakir was so handsome with a perfect face like Hrithik Roshan. How could she be unhappy living in such close proximity to such beauty. His village, too, sounded idyllic, situated by the banks of the river Manas close to the sanctuary where wildlife and exotic plants and trees grew in abundance. By then her life had started to revolve around dreams of the village faraway in Assam. She was all ready to wear different clothes while she visited there and Zakir had said that she would be called Zarina. How lovely that sounded—Zakir and Zarina. For a long time she sat and dreamed of a new life, far away, in a village by the river.

Her reverie was rudely broken by Hmingthani's voice, 'Come fast you silly girl. There are more people for tea today. Here, take this money and run to the bakery. Get a dozen patties, six chicken and six pork, a dozen cheese sandwiches and a plum cake. My cake flopped! Run…'

Mawii gathered her still wet hair in a chignon on top of her head and tightened her puan, tucked it in and ran. The hair clip gave way and her hair tumbled down to her shoulders. Putting the five hundred rupee note between her teeth she plaited her hair loosely and then put it up again. Kapi Lalpeki had warned her that if ever she saw or heard complaints about her untidy hair style she would have to go for a boy crop. Zakir had told her that that was totally unacceptable to him, much as he loved her. Mawii had promised that she would never ever cut her hair.

She hurried along the roads that led to the bakery. There were many strollers window-shopping and trying out clothes and clips and colourful shoes. Mawii eyed them from the corner of her eye as she knew she had to hurry back, suppressing a smile as she thought of her little suitcase filled with the goodies which she had bought from the money she had saved all these months.

'Such dull clothes,' Hmingthani had remarked when she saw them and sniffed imperiously, walking away.

'These are for there. They do not like women in too bright clothes, Nu,' countered Mawii.

'How does it matter to you?' she said softly but Hmingthani heard.

'Don't be rude. And this talk about 'there' and 'them' makes me sick. Do not answer me back. You are younger and you should be grateful that I have not told anyone about your shocking plans. As it is I sweat and pant when I think of what I have to face on the day you run away with that vai. Oh God! I may even have a stroke. What a plight. Don't you feel sorry for me? I will have to lie and say I knew nothing. Oh God! Will I be able to do that? Maybe I will never be allowed to enter the church again!'

'For what?' It was Mawii's turn to be shaken.

'Everyone will think that I had been conniving with that vai.'

'I am not the first to marry one and I won't be the last.'

Then Mawii saw Hmingthani cry, tears rolling down her fat cheeks lined with the ravines of dreams gone wrong.

Mawii brushed her thoughts aside and rushed back with the cakes and patties just in time. The guests had just walked in. Such smart couples, Kapi Rulupuii and her husband, Kapu Jimmy, his brother, Kapu Ron and his stunning wife, Kapi Sinteii who sang like Taylor Swift. Kapi Rulupuii wore a puan of grey and turquoise, the typical weave of the Hmar tribe, Kapi Sinteii wore a pink dress which flowed in waves down to her calves, decent enough for a visit such as this. She sang in concerts, weddings and in radio programs. She was a star. Mawii felt good serving a celebrity and thinking of the many songs she sang like a diva, unsurpassed, transporting you to another world where love reigned supreme.

That night it rained incessantly and Hmingthani dragged her cot away from the window next to Mawii. As she snored away Mawii thought of Zakir in his makeshift accommodation which he shared along with the other workers from the plains. Last week one had died in his sleep, he had drunk too much. He was Kundan Prasad, the Bihari, the most educated of the lot. Zakir had told her that Kundan would roam around at night and sometimes would bring pork and rice for dinner, too drunk to be concerned about Zakir and his clan. 'You are a Brahmin, Kundan and you are eating meat?' Zakir had once chided him. To which a very drunk and very merry Kundan Prasad Sharma slurred,

'What did contractor shir say? Huh? When in Rome do ash Romansh do. Hah! So good English, na?' Zakir said he couldn't help but smile. Kundan was an endearing soul. Zakir and all the workers wept copiously at the funeral.

'Mawii, you idiot, what is all this about not eating this and that and not drinking? The Muslims do eat this and that and drink and smoke and are so horny they keep four wives and breed like...Ugh! Horrible! You don't even watch TV...they are horrible people blowing up the whole world. Silly girl, Mawii. Biaka loves you so much. He is Mizo and a good Christian. Has such a good job in the beauty parlour. Best hair cuts in the whole of Aizawl, that means the whole of Northeast. He even has a house in Zarkot. A small house—so what? His mother is such a lovely woman and she sings like an angel. You should hear her sing. Have you ever heard her sing? You silly girl, you are not even listening to me!' This had been the after-dinner chat while clearing the kitchen.

Hmingthani lit a cigarette to ease her discomfort. She had seen Zakir once. He was tall and wiry with a face like a film star. She understood how Mawii felt but she felt weighed down by her sense of responsibility. How she could allow her own girl to run away with a vai and that, too, a Muslim! Not all Muslims were bad and most, certainly, were not terrorists. Her favourite shop in the market was owned by one family, the Ahmeds, a grocery-cum-utensil shop which she and her family had patronized for generations. On their festivals, steaming meat fried rice called biryani would be sent and sometimes, the most delicious rice pudding which they called kheer. She felt, however, that she must do her utmost to prevent Mawii from running away. Jesus would certainly reward her. Delighted with the thought, her face split into a smile.

'Mawii, think carefully. Biaka is meant for you. He looks right for you. Maybe you will produce a daughter as beautiful as Kapi Sinteii, there is a slight resemblance between the two, they are related you know. Your daughter will also sing like an angel or like those many singers you like…with names I can neither remember nor pronounce! Isn't this enough to be happy? I was so happy with my Lalbuanga. We were so happy in New Delhi in Mizoram House. He was the best cook in the world.' Tears streamed down her cheeks as she remembered her after-work walks down almost empty roads outside the building with her late husband. Cars whizzed by, so many different types of cars, so many colours, shapes and sizes. They would watch for a while, awed and excited, especially when the long black Rolls Royce of the wealthy neighbours would glide out of the gate and down the tree-lined boulevard like a queen. In winter, after lunch, they would go to the park nearby after church, dressed so well, people smiled at them, some would wish them. Until the day the lady with a poodle stopped and asked them where they came from.

'From Mizoram. You reach there via Assam. It is close to Myanmar,' explained Lalbuanga. He had done it so often, the second and third sentence flowed out in one breath.

'It's in India?' the lady asked, tugging at her poodle.

'Yes,' replied Hmingthani. Just one word

'What are you doing in Delhi?' poodle lady asked, undeterred.

'We cook in Mizoram House.'

'Oh! Oh! How interesting! Er...what do you cook?'

'Food,' replied Hmingthani and she walked away, her nose in the air, her lips shut tight.

That was the last time they ever acknowledged each other—the two ladies in the park.

'It's a relief actually, Mami. Thank you,' Lalbuanga said, patting his wife on her shoulder as the lady with the poodle walked past. Back home he would have put his arm around her and given her a hug.

And then one day while returning from a party in Gurgaon with a minister, Buanga died in an accident. He was not even supposed to go but the driver was his friend and asked him to accompany him. 'It's so boring waiting for these guys' party to get over. Come, at least we can chat. You have no work. Come on.'

Hmingthani was about to cry but she didn't. She said to Mawii, 'Delhi was nice. You could have run away with a vai from Delhi, you silly girl. There are so many right here where your Zakir is working. Not exactly from Delhi but close by, here and there.'

Mawii did not think so but dared not say a word. She had heard of the North Indian men, about how awful they were—lecherous as hell and with absolutely no respect for women. A woman was a mere chattel and sex mate and a bouncing board when they were frustrated, angry and drunk. Then they would beat the shit out of the woman or go and rape and torture and mutilate a woman till all the muck had seeped out of their sick minds. That was what she had heard about the majority of the men in the north.

She did not know that Hmingthani had just bitten her lip as she said this because it was such a goddamned lie. She never complained to Buanga but, oh boy, she really had to fight back to ward off the pawing chowkidar, the sexual touch in the kitchen as she passed by bearers, the manager who would call her to give instructions but would go beyond duties and keep chatting, salivating all the while, looking at her breasts. One day, she realized that she was no longer proud of her womanhood. She felt ashamed and nervous. She had decided to tell Buanga to ask for a transfer but then she thought, what the hell, she would show these men a thing or two. She would fight her own battle. And she did.

The opportunity presented itself just like that on a fine winter evening. She remembered it with much clarity and much satisfaction. She had stepped out for a walk in the evening all by herself, stick in hand after a most infuriating afternoon after lunch when Sukhi, the dhobi had brushed against her chest on the stairs while taking up some clothes. Just like that—grinning away after the deed was done, while her breasts felt hot and gritty like angry cats. So that evening during her usual walking hour at sundown, she went out of the gate, swinging a walking stick casually, head held high. One would think she was just out on an evening walk with a stick in hand in case she encountered a stray dog. She had not gone far when she sighted Ravinder, the dhobi's cousin, and a darwan in the bungalow three houses away. She went straight at him from the back and pierced his behind as hard as she could. Ravinder screamed and turning around was about to attack her when he felt a slap on his face, hard and strong, and a beating on his right shoulder. Hmingthani stood in front of him, nostrils flaring, 'You touch me and I will file a police complaint about your lecherous cousin, Sukhi. If his wife has no tits it isn't my problem. I am tired of him trying to grab mine. I would have beaten the shit out of him but I don't want my husband to lose his job here. He likes Delhi. The damn manager would not support us—that Punjabi—he will say it is my fault and maybe he will even try to grab me too. Thoo, you disgusting men.'

Ravinder stared at her as she walked away. His bottom was hurting but how could he let her see that. That night when he reached home, he socked his younger brother, Sukhi, hard in the face, and walked away shouting, 'Your wife's tits are good enough for you, bastard. My back is hurting because of you. Dare you touch that Mizo woman again. Sala.' Ravinder tossed around in bed thinking of his attacker's slit eyes flashing and her determined step as she walked away fearlessly. He felt a stirring in his body as he touched his wife. She responded, pursing her lips and clenching her teeth as he entered her.

Hmingthani, totally unaware of a new admirer in

the vicinity, revelled in her newfound confidence and enjoyed the entire winter in Delhi, not knowing it would be her last.

'Yes, I have loved and lost but with my own community. It's different. It is respectable. It is safe, Mawii.'

The guests were leaving and Mawii cleared the table and piled the cups and saucers near the sink. Slowly she started to wash them, deep in thought. Tonight she would sneak off to meet Zakir. She had called him a few days back when she had longed for his embrace, thirsting for his touch. He said he would wait just outside the Solomon Temple. The other workers would have been gone by then on their evening jaunts and most people would be indoors watching TV as it was serial time. Mawii knew there would be no dinner to be served after that heavy tea. Kapi Lalpeki and her cousin would only have a cup of Horlicks and her niece would sip a brandy and have a light snack.

'Nu, I want to go to see my cousin in…I just want to talk things over with her. Please, please tell Kapi to let me go. I will be back by ten. Please.'

Hmingthani looked into the young girl's eyes and refused to see the lie.

'Okay. Go carefully.'

It had rained for a while earlier in the evening, one of those showers that come and go suddenly like a dream one can't remember. The streets were lit up and empty as Mawii walked not looking right or left and not too fast. That would have invited attention from the drunks.

No one walked fast in the night in Aizawl for it was time to unwind and slow dance your fatigue away. Some cars whizzed past her, probably after an early supper and musical soiree at the home of a friend or relative, a popular pastime in this hill town. She kept walking, passing half-closed shops and houses with curtains drawn and the sound of TV and some chattering inside—happy sounds. For a split second Mawii wondered what she would be watching once she was in Assam amidst different people, so very different people. Young kids under the awnings of a bank were sitting and smoking dope, some already high on stronger stuff. Mawii bit her lip and fought back her tears, thinking of her two brothers who died of an overdose. Then she sighted the church shining like a beacon amidst a sea of rooftops. She hurried and was almost at the building where Zakir worked, near the jacaranda where he said he would be waiting. He had said, 'Hari would be out by then and we can sit in the room and have some time to ourselves... Am looking forward, Mawii.' His voice was soft and hoarse with emotion in his halting Mizo with that strong Assamese accent. She felt weak in the knees just thinking of him and she felt a kind of fear and apprehension too. She had traversed alone for four almost deserted kilometers to an unfamiliar locality in the dead of night. In Aizawl most people slept by ten. She eyed the stout pillar of the ornate gate where Zakir usually emerged from, with that smile which could only be his. I will wait, she thought, I will wait for that smile, Zakir. I will wait for it with this flutter in my heart and the weakening in my knees.

A breeze blew past and a few jacaranda blossoms fell on the ground and on her head and it continued, unabated, as a whole spray came down like confetti.

She was enjoying this strange nocturnal ballet when she saw Hari coming up from the compound of the building walking quickly, stealthily. Her heart sank. She clung to the jacarandas that she had caught in her hand and waited.

'He had to leave for Assam immediately. Some paperwork had to be completed otherwise he won't be able to vote. You know how important that is. The elections are in early May. He tried to call. He couldn't get through. See…he even left his mobile behind to show you he tried to call. See, six times!'

Mawii took the mobile and without looking pressed it close to her heart. She looked at Hari, her eyes filled with unshed tears. She kept looking at him. This was the first time that she looked at him. She was never comfortable to look at a vai and Hari was so vai with his big eyes, dark skin and almost six foot frame. He was from Bihar—God alone knew how far that was but they once had a funny leader called Lallu. Everyone talked about him and told funny stories about him. His wife was also an MLA. That meant he was not bad at all. He gave his wife a chance not like other vais.

'Hari, what exactly did Zakir say?'

'Arre, it was like this. His uncle called last night and said he must come, all of them in fact. They have put their papers in proper order and identification has to be done again. You know…so many illegal immigrants.'

'But Hari, Zakir is not, no?'

'No, no. His grandfather came long ago during Indira Gandhi's time. They are well settled near Barpeta.'

'Is it a nice place, Hari? The village by the river?'

'I have not been there but Zakirbhai's village is close to the river Manas. It is always nice to be near a river. Not too close of course because when it rains…'

'Hari, tell me about your village by the river in Bihar…' She wanted to prolong the night and the inevitability of what she would have to face.

'Not Bihar. East Uttar Pradesh in a village called Kheri. That was where I grew up, in a zamindar's farm. They were Sikhs and very kind. All through the year we swam and during the season we caught fish. The big catch would go to the kothi and the rest we would keep. Well, when they were away in Delhi and Chandigarh then you can imagine, ha ha ha…'

'But Bihar?'

'Then one day the river decided to change course… at night while we were asleep it came in a whoosh into our hut. It swept away my three sisters and two brothers. They were never found. My parents out of shock and grief left for Gorakhpur to an uncle who worked in a sugar cane factory. My parents are still there, in their sixties now, working.'

'Has the Manas ever flooded and taken people away?'

'No, but the Brahmaputra has…'

'Okay, I will go now.'

'Here, keep his mobile.'

'No. You keep it. He will call. You said two weeks,

after the elections. So I will wait and see...' Mawii smiled but her eyes had a faraway look as if she was somewhere else as she walked away.

Then all of a sudden she turned back and said, 'Hari, I am sending a message to Zakir. You keep the mobile... carefully. You save it and store it. Do not delete it even by mistake.'

She took out her mobile from her bag and typed, 'Zakir, don't worry. Am fine. I will always remember the times we spent together. One day, I will visit you even as a toothless grandmother. I want to see your village by the river. I love you very much but it is not necessary that people who love each other stay together. In fact they seldom do...'

She gave back the mobile to Hari and fled into the night.

THE LIMP

The Limp

The day after the funeral he suddenly realized that his limp was gone. He wanted to share this discovery with Rumi, his wife, but decided against it. Miracles, like secrets, were best left unshared.

It was the first Sunday of the new millennium and, in any case, on Sundays shops do not open in Police Bazaar. Nipendro Roy was luxuriating in the winter sun, his mind alternating between remembering and forgetting.

Nipen had had a good season, most of the goods in his crockery shop had sold out during Christmas. He smiled as he sat in his twelve feet by ten feet patch of green on an old cane chair that creaked every time he shifted. He enjoyed the sound now so familiar and reassuring. At one corner of the garden a tulsi shrub sat comfortably, knowing it was the chosen one. Much to his wife Rumi's consternation, he had refused to grow flowers like everyone did in Shillong. After all, they did not have flowers in their garden in Sonamgunj. He stretched his legs and twisted his toes playfully, silently celebrating the fact that, miraculously, his twenty-year-old limp had disappeared. He watched Rumi walk down the hill in her pastel saree with a flowery print. No more plain cottons with bright borders like the rest of the community. She now blended with the locals, at least in what she wore including her practiced smile that stretched across her face like a cut. Their son had left for

Australia to do his MBA the previous autumn. Letters sailed into the letter box every week packed with news, much to Rumi's delight. She would read the letters out aloud again and again until the day Nipen remarked, 'I don't know why he is so proud about learning to eat with forks and spoons—it is like making love by proxy.'

He couldn't really figure out why he shut her up like that. Perhaps it was because he missed his son so much—even more so after his parents passed away. Baba had advised him not to go for the new-fangled, one-child idea. He could hear Baba's voice floating through his mind, 'Your Ma couldn't have more children but you can, I am sure.' But even Rumi couldn't. That was the destiny of the family. That was what Ma had said when he told her. Just a few words but as usual so gently put. Nipen had immediately felt convinced and comforted.

So many years have passed, Nipendro smiled, as he sat on the old cane chair revelling in the fact that he no longer limped. He remembered the day he got that limp twenty years ago. It was no ordinary day, not for a twenty-year-old son of an immigrant family still trying to understand a world they chose to live in where instead of plains there were hills and instead of sunset yodels there were church bells that rent the air like war cries.

He remembered crossing the little bridge that spanned the stream that divided the lower part of the colony from the upper more crowded area where he used to live. He leaned hard against the old pine tree, feeling secure by the roughness and immovability of the ancient bark. He shook his leg and muttered, 'Come on leg, straighten up you silly fool, come on, come on.' He said it in English so that the passersby would not be able to determine which community he belonged to. He had heard that at the moment Marwaris and Punjabis were not targeted, only Bengalis and Nepalese were.

'Come on, leg. Come on, we are going home.' He certainly did not want his parents to fret and panic over the limp and send him to the doctor again. The limp had nothing to do with doctors and medicines. He had confirmed that with the homeopath the day it happened. He knew it himself anyway.

It was on the day that he had gone to see Bimola mashi, his mother's elder sister, the day after her house almost got burnt down. When he reached her house she was peeling potatoes in the kitchen. He touched her feet and waited for her to say something but she didn't. She kept on peeling potatoes. His cousin, Soma, a college student who lived with her was washing clothes in the garden. The water gushed out strong and aggressive from a rather startled tap that stood on functional cement flooring in one corner. He turned the tap and lessened the flow. She smiled weakly and said, 'Nipenda, thanks to Kong Tis we were saved. I have been telling pishi that we should move. We should go where most of our people live, like your locality for example, but you know pishi! Anyway, we got saved thanks to her best friend, Kong Tis. Nipenda, you should have seen, Nipenda, you should have seen her. She simply stood at our gate. She stood there without saying a word, not a word, but none of those chaps dared to even look sideways at our house. They were carrying tins of kerosene. You should have seen Kong Tis, she leaned on our gate with both hands on the top of it. She kept chewing her kwai as if that is what she does every morning—leaning on a little wooden gate of a cottage inhabited by Bengalis. It was amazing, Nipenda—such a nice lady and so strong, a true Khasi woman. But still—why did we have to come here where the locals do not like us? They feel we are taking away their jobs and opportunities in the offices especially. But there are exams for all this, aren't there? There is nothing unfair, surely. They have shops too like we have. Bara Bazaar is only for the locals and my…it is so huge—the biggest market I have ever seen.'

Nipen's eyes had smarted as the wind rushed through the pines and he could smell the aroma of wet trees and an approaching spring. 'This is home where the pines are. This is home,' he whispered.

'Indeed not, Nipenda, indeed not. Let us not fool ourselves. Why did we come here? Why? I want to go back to Sonamgunj and bathe in the ponds while Thakurma sings—*sohag chand badoni nacho to dekhi/ Bala nacho to dekhi/ Balo nacho to dekhi…*Why did we come here, Nipenda? Why?'

'For a better life, Soma, for a better life.'

'I don't care. It was scary. I want to be uneducated, I want to be poor as long as I can live without fear. Why can't I have a choice? Why do you men always chose for us?'

'There is no human being who lives without fear,

some kind of fear, men more than women. Only saints live without fear.'

'What do you mean? Why are you quiet? What do you mean?'

'I was thinking of the answer—the right answer—otherwise you will jump down my throat!'

Soma laughed and her eyes lit up like lamps.

'Well, Soma, I think all people who live on alien land live with fear—the degree varies—but fear sits on us piggy-back.'

'Oh Nipenda, how terrible! I want to go back. I want to wear cotton frocks and skirts again and bathe in the ponds and hear Thakurma sing—*Sohag chand badono dhoni nacho...*'

'Stop dreaming. Thakurma is dead and you are too old to wear frocks and that's that. Now let me go across and thank Kong Tis.'

Soma opened her mouth to say something but she stopped. She started to rub the clothes with unnecessary vigour as tears rushed down her face and she watched him go.

Nipendro's grandfather had come up to these hills in the 1930s as a junior to a reputed lawyer who decided to come up because his wife had TB. The doctors had said the only cure was the pine-scented air of the Khasi Hills. So many other families had also migrated to this paradise where they could set up shops and practices and eke a decent living.

As Nipen walked away towards Kong Tis' house he ruminated that it was probably the hundredth time he would be thanking Kong Tishina Lyngdoh in the twenty-five years that he had known her. As a gangly lad of thirteen, newly arrived from Sonamgunj, he had visited Bimola mashi with his parents. He remembered the tedious conversation of loss and longing suddenly interrupted by the entrance of a huge Khasi woman carrying a basket of oranges. For Nipen it was like a sudden burst of sunshine, the wide warm smile and the hug dissipated all the awkwardness and diffidence that had clung to him like a second skin. He felt his generously oiled shock of hair shone like a true hero's and his oversized, sloppy shoes transformed into a fashion statement. Then the watch on his eighteenth birthday was given by her, the watch his parents could not afford. Somehow Bimola mashi had managed to confide in Kong Tis about his birthday wish in one of her over-the-fence-conversations. Kong Tis did not give him the exact one. That would have been indelicate. She had chosen one that was a couple of hundred rupees cheaper but a rectangular one all the same, perfect and clear with a black dial. The way she gave it to him, not making a big show out of it, made it even more special—not typical. He remembered that he was biting into a piping hot singhara when Kong Tis flounced into the room and announced that she had got the contract to build a new border road near Dawki 'and to celebrate this big event with another big event I thought giving a present to an eighteen-year-old from across the border from Dawki would be just perfect.' Amidst claps and cheers she gave him the watch and her famous bear hug. He touched her feet and then spluttered nervously, 'Thank you for not stuffing a shondesh into my mouth.' Everyone laughed as he strapped the watch on his hand.

That was so many years ago. Right now another memory flooded his mind. The day he went to check on Bimola mashi after a night of carnage in the city. That was the day he developed the limp.

Nipen remembered that Kong Tis' house looked desolate. It was lunch time. The ground floor which housed the office and godowns was empty. The upper floors which accommodated her large family of a sister and brother and a host of nieces and nephews also seemed empty and silent. The many windows glowered down at him like sightless eyes. He was about to press the bell when he suddenly realized that she was standing at the doorway, filling the dark space like a Rembrandt. She was not her cheerful, bouncy self but had put on a grim and serious air that hung on her like a borrowed dress. Maybe he should not have come and Soma was right in trying to stop him, it was too soon after the tension in the town. He sensed that there was something wrong.

Slowly he saw Kong Tis lift her hand and then shake her index finger. No. No. Not a step further. Her hand moving quickly shoving him off like an unwanted fly. He started to move away and before he did he looked at her eyes gleaming and hard like marbles in a frozen pond. He walked away and turned again and stared at her and as he turned to go he saw her eyes soften. She knew he had understood that there were local boys inside waiting for that opportunity to attack. He stepped into the gravel. His head was throbbing and he thought he was going to blank out but somehow managed to contain himself. He headed quickly towards the gate and then, suddenly, he realized that he was limping. Bimola mashi took him to a doctor immediately who whispered conspiratorially to her that her nephew seemed to have been through some trauma. He prescribed him some medicines and taught him some exercises. A few days later he felt better but every now and again when he felt nervous it would return and he would go back to his medicines and exercises until one day, he realized he actually enjoyed limping. It was a funny kind of release and it gave him a special character and reminded him of Kong Tis. After a while his parents, too, gave up worrying and attributed it all to a family eccentricity they seemed to be familiar with.

Now so many years later the town was calm and his limp was gone. And he could see Rumi in her flowery pastel coloured saree going to the market, not in dark cottons with typical borders and worn above the ankles. 'Are you preparing for the floods, Bimola?' he could hear Kong Tis asking Bimola mashi and both of them would collapse with laughter. He could hear all that with the wind rushing through the pines.

Yesterday was Kong Tis' funeral. He had thrown some earth on her coffin along with all her relatives as it was lowered onto the ground. Then he closed his eyes and whispered, 'Goodbye Tis mashi. You will rest in peace. You were a good soul.'

Soma had come too with her husband. They had come up from Assam where they both taught in a school. He had heard of Kong Tis. She was his wife's undisputed heroine. Besides he had never been to a Christian funeral and was curious. They stood a little apart from everyone like special displays in a shop.

Nipen closed his eyes in his ten by six feet garden alternating between remembering and forgetting and smiled contentedly...as he inhaled the aroma of wet pines and treasured memories of days gone by.

Acknowledgements

Thank you, Neena De, for convincing me not to tuck away this manuscript like I have so many others, because you felt this is one story that had never been told...and must be told. That was how I made that trip to Delhi.

Prof Moon Moon Mazumdar who agreed that it was a unique and brave literary work and must see the light of day.

Geert Linnebank—a brilliant mind and a voracious reader whose praise gave me the encouragement to carry on. Thanks too to Roshmi Goswami, John Potts and Minnie Khadim Ali for your generous reading of the book, and for saying you are looking forward to a sequel...and perhaps there will be one!

Thank you, Ravi Singh and Renuka Chatterjee of Speaking Tiger, for keeping *Shadow Men* alive, and to Urvashi Butalia who called it 'a little gem'.

Shadow Men is a personal viewpoint—articulating the unspoken, the unheard and reaching out for solutions.

Once you know the problem, solutions are but a step away...

ALSO IN SPEAKING TIGER

THE SLEEPWALKER'S DREAM

Dhrubajyoti Borah

June, along with Ron and several other insurgents, is fleeing their hideout in Bhutan after an army attack. With them is their injured, unconscious leader who is unlikely to survive the ordeal of their journey towards the Assam border. They carry him on a stretcher over the treacherous terrain of the Himalayan foothills, the ominous and brooding presence of the mountains a constant reminder of their own defencelessness. With winter upon them they desperately need to find a temporary shelter. Miraculously, their leader emerges from his coma and is able to guide them to a cave where he had earlier created a 'safe house' with supplies of food and other essentials.

For June, a young woman trapped by events beyond her control into becoming an insurgent in troubled Assam, the journey is a test of her endurance and dedication. As the only woman in the group she sometimes feels alienated but is determined to make the best of a situation that is extremely tough for all of them. She does sentry duty like all the others and keeps herself in good physical shape. But her memories keep taking her back to her long-lost family, her village, her innocent childhood and the tragic circumstances under which she had become an insurgent. Ron, too, is flooded by his own memories of his boyhood and the turbulent early days of passionate commitment and high adventure. With a deep understanding of human psychology and keen attention to detail, Dhrubajyoti Borah traces the journey of Ron, June and the other insurgents towards an elusive freedom and an uncertain future.

272 pp. | ₹350/-

ALSO IN SPEAKING TIGER

A FULL NIGHT'S THIEVERY
STORIES

Mitra Phukan

A musician never realized the truth of the saying 'Music is a harsh taskmaster' until his beloved instrument exacts the highest sacrifice. An unfaithful husband is baffled: his wife grows more and more perfect until she literally becomes the goddess of plenty. A loving mother is naturally distraught at the kidnapping of her son by insurgents...or is she? And Modon Sur, with the spoils of a full night's thievery in tow, finds himself in a sticky situation on a black amavasya night.

In this collection, Mitra Phukan sounds the rhythms of contemporary Assamese society, deftly weaving universal themes of love, loss and ageing with some of the issues facing the region: militancy, witchcraft, and the breakdown of traditional ways of life. Her stories acutely depict people's struggles to relate to each other across vast social gulfs and within the intricacies of family and love. Intimate, allusive, and wryly observed, *A Full Night's Thievery* is a finely drawn portrait of humanity by one of the most prominent literary voices in Assam today.

232 pp. | ₹299/-

ALSO IN SPEAKING TIGER

THE REAL MR BARKOTOKI

Shisir Basumatari

A young man is troubled by recurring dreams of visiting a mysterious Munin Barkotoki, 'a God-fearing man', every night. Later at a scrap dealer's shop, when he accidentally unearths a book by the very same person, he is shocked and intrigued. The 'man of his dreams' happened to be very real, and a noted Assamese writer and critic.

Determined to get to the bottom of this mystery, he teams up with his friend, Capt D., and Dr Das, a psychologist, to piece together the identity of this reclusive, enigmatic figure and why he continues to haunt his dreams. Through his hypnosis sessions with Dr Das, and rifling through Barkotoki's diaries, speeches, audio recordings, he attempts to decipher the brilliant mind of Assamese literature. On the way he uncovers his quirks, such as his famous walk to the District Library in Guwahati at exactly the same time every day, his atrocious handwriting, and his staunch literary activism during British rule.

But still, each step that they take leads them to a dead end. This leaves them with no choice but to undertake a journey into the afterlife. Encountering ghostly magistrates, cars flying through time and space, missing plutonium on the Nanda Devi, *The Real Mr Barkotoki* is a trippy adventure and a visual treat. Distinctly illustrated in the vein of Joe Sacco's gritty realism, this graphic novel brings to life one of Assam's best known and most mystifying figures in an entertaining noir-style mystery.

184 pp. | ₹499/-